THE PHYSICIANS

To be 'Central trained' meant something special...

The relationship between Nurse Anne Heseltine, a young widow, and Dr Michael Vanstone had been a strange one. Several times Anne had felt they were on the verge of a deeper understanding, when Michael had drawn back, afraid to commit himself. Hospital gossip also linked his name with that of Jennifer Ramsay, a pretty student nurse who was obviously out to catch him – and Anne herself knew that she was loved by Bill Barham. When the Professorship at the Central became vacant, Anne realised that the two men were becoming serious rivals – in work and in love...

THE PHYSICIANS

The Physicians

by

Elizabeth Harrison

Dales Large Print Books
Long Preston, North Yorkshire,
BD23 4ND, England.

British Library Cataloguing in Publication Data.

Harrison, Elizabeth
    The physicians.

    A catalogue record of this book is
    available from the British Library

    ISBN   978-1-84262-729-7 pbk

First published in Great Britain by Ward Lock and Co. Ltd.

Cover illustration © Ilona Wellmann by arrangement with
Arcangel Images

The moral right of the author has been asserted

Published in Large Print 2010 by arrangement with
Watson, Little Ltd.

Dales Large Print is an imprint of Library Magna Books Ltd.

Printed and bound in Great Britain by
T.J. (International) Ltd., Cornwall, PL28 8RW

Chapter 1

Anne Heseltine was in love with Michael Vanstone. She imagined that no one knew this but herself, though here she was mistaken. She and Michael both worked at the Central London Hospital, and the staff there had a quick eye for love affairs.

Michael Vanstone was brilliant, most people agreed about that, though some of his colleagues accused him of being remote and aloof. It was true that he was sceptical, cool, analytical. What need he had for human relationships was usually satisfied in his work in the clinics, the wards and his consulting rooms. Then, too, he hated to see suffering and be unable to help. Yet even today, with all the resources of modern medicine, as they existed at the Central, one of London's great teaching hospitals, there was often little he could do to alleviate the misery of the incurable. His only remedy was to refrigerate his emotions. They had never been overwhelming, and with this constant discipline they dwindled further.

Women frequently loved him. Partly because he was appealingly good looking – tall, slight, and dark, with a narrow humorous mouth, and soft brown eyes.

His love affairs had never yet come to anything. He was too quizzical and doubtful, and if a flicker was roused in him he was apt to quench it with a douche of deliberate cynicism.

Inadvertently, he was inclined to promise more than he was prepared to give. He would have been horrified to learn this, for he always intended to play fair, never meant to offer more than he could fulfil. But even he had his moments – and love, affection, desire would burst into urgent life. The trouble was that he easily cooled off again.

This had happened many times between him and Anne Heseltine. At last, though, what she felt sure was to be the long-awaited love affair between them finally got off – after a phenomenally slow start – at the house-warming party Meg and Andy Taussig held in the spring.

The Taussigs' new house in Hampstead was not large, but it was charming, and Meg had furnished it with modern oiled teak and deep leather chairs. The living-room had windows from floor to ceiling, while beside the fireplace, steps led down to the lower level of the dining-room, where glass doors gave on to a small patio, with whitewashed walls, a pergola, and a high gate to the road.

When Anne arrived at the party, Miss Glossop, Matron of the Central London Hospital, was standing formidably by the door, and her first words linked Michael Vanstone firmly – and alarmingly, as far as Anne was concerned – with Jennifer Ramsay. Jennifer could be seen on the far side of the room, wearing one of the newest smocks in fondant pink, with matching shoes. She was talking to Michael. His dark head was bent, her lively young face upturned to him, fresh and glowing. They were both engrossed.

'What a charming couple they make, don't they?' Miss Glossop's voice announced at Anne's side. The remark was guaranteed to spoil her evening. Was there anything in it, she wondered? Remarks of this kind, rumours, were not new to her. Surely Jennifer was too young for Michael? In her second year as a student nurse at the Central, surely she could be no more than nineteen? Michael, an established consultant, was by now in his late thirties.

They both came towards the door.

Jennifer greeted Miss Glossop and Anne with her unfailing poise, and said, 'Night duty, worse luck. I only looked in with Mummy and Daddy.' Sir Alexander Ramsay, Professor of Medicine at the Central, and Lady Ramsay, could be seen in the middle of a busy group over by the window. 'I must rush,' Jennifer added, and waved a hand vaguely in the direction of her parents.

'I'm driving her down,' Michael said to Anne. 'I'll be back in a minute,' he added, and gave her a look she would have thought significant, had Miss Glossop not been beforehand with her remark.

'What a nice child that is,' she now said indefatigably, still planted by the doorway. Anne agreed politely, and wandered on into the room, looking for Meg Taussig. Meg had immediately asked her to stay on for dinner, and added that she had already invited Michael Vanstone. This restored Anne's hopefulness, and she began to enjoy the party.

An hour or two later, while Meg and Andy were seeing off the last of their guests, Michael and Anne collected glasses and ashtrays, and made vague attempts to restore some sort of order to the big living-room.

Meg came back into the room, pushed back her fluffy dark hair, and took a deep breath of relaxation. 'What blissful quiet,' she said. 'The place sounded like the playground of – of a secondary modern school in a particularly tough area near the docks. Why is it that the moment they have a glass in their hands, they all scream at each other?' She glanced at the clock. 'There's a joint in the oven. Should be just about ready. They all went fairly punctually, thank heavens. Everywhere's in a pig mess, I'm afraid. We'll simply have to eat in the middle of it.'

Michael's lips twitched. Anne knew why. It would not be the first time they had eaten good food in the middle of a pig mess with the Taussigs. The new house, for all its Scandinavian furniture and Japanese grasscloth wall coverings, was unmistakably a Taussig dwelling place. She and Michael caught one another's eye, and Anne, as always, felt completely at home with him. Whatever Miss Glossop chose to imply, this understanding between them must be significant, must surely lead somewhere? Her loneliness was coming to an end.

Anne had been nineteen when she had married Tim Heseltine. They were both students. They had lived together for five tempestuous, impecunious years, and then he had been killed, climbing in the Dolomites. Anne had taken the job she now held at the Central, and life had gone inexorably on, slowly becoming bearable again. Recently, for the first time since Tim's death, she had felt her emotions spring into new life whenever Michael Vanstone had been with her.

She was a tall, willowy girl, with blonde hair piled round her head, fine bones and a narrow face, which could seem beautiful or pinched, according to her mood, and vivid blue eyes. She looked sophisticated and often elegant, and people thought her calm and self-assured. In fact, of the two of them, the soft and pliable Meg, whom all her friends considered to be so much at the mercy of Andy, was not only more confident but far better able to take care of herself.

Neither of them, though, had been lucky with men, Meg's mother was accustomed to complain. Meg had married Andy Taussig when she was in her early twenties. (She might, her mother lamented, 'have had anyone'.) It was only now, ten years later, that she had been able for the first time to give up work (she had been a ward sister at the

Central) to run her house. Andy and she were, if not prosperous now, at least comfortably off, for the first time since what everyone had, rightly, prophesied would be a disastrous marriage. The new house in Hampstead was materially different from their earlier squalid lodgings. Centrally heated, double-glazed, split level, the latest gadgets – Meg had gone to town once she had started. All this was a long way from the cheap furnished rooms the Taussigs used to live in, thick with cigarette smoke, deep in dust, drab, littered with emptied cups, ashtrays brimming over, apple cores, notebooks, cast-off clothing, shoes, ties, collars. Andy dropped whatever he no longer wanted wherever he happened to be standing, and snarled if Meg rushed to pick it up.

'We've sold my shares for the deposit,' Meg had been explaining this evening to anyone who cared to listen, 'and bought the furniture out of our savings. So there are only repayments, and Andy can easily meet those out of his income.' Pleased, she failed to notice eyes that took on a calculating gleam, as they darted about pricing house and furniture. Those who were less worldly, whose eyes failed to glaze with auctioneer's intensity, were those who would never, at any price, accept Andy. They registered only disgust at Meg's news, one more black mark against Andy, and went into corners to mutter together that at last that dreadful man seemed to have got his hands on all of poor Meg's money, on top of everything else.

Andy Taussig, now forty, was marked by the struggle his life had been, and marked for the worse. As a boy, he had been trained as a pianist, had been brought up in a comfortable middle-class home in Vienna, his father an orchestral conductor who had never quite achieved international standing. Andy was to do this. The family had great hopes for him. He was to be a concert pianist of world renown. Whether they were right, or hopelessly over-optimistic, would never be known, for he was only sixteen when Hitler overran Austria, and their happy, easy life dissolved, vanished as if it had never been.

Andy's father died. Shot while escaping, as they called it. His mother went to the gas chambers, but not before Andy had seen her scrubbing pavements outside their flat, to the jeers of the young Nazi hooligans standing by, armed and powerful.

This had been the beginning of the hate that bubbled still in Andy, hate powerless then to find expression, and locked with fear and shame in his heart.

'Try not to mind, darling,' his mother had said, torn more by Andy's stricken gaze than by her own imminent danger. The words rang lovingly down the years, feeding his bitterness, emphasising his desolation.

Ten years later, in his middle twenties, Andy Taussig came out of a camp for displaced persons, penniless, friendless. By now he had a sardonic sense of humour (he had been a gay little boy, once), together with a mass of undigested grudges, and a repressed yearning for love and affection. His most outstanding characteristic, though, was his instinct for survival, and his ability to put his own needs before all else. Perhaps he might have found his way, eventually, out of the hideous confusion he was in, if he had been able to return to his music. This could have opened him, allowed him to discharge the poison that festered. But he cut himself off from anything to do with it. He had been forced to do without his family, without love. He would never look back. Some dogged obstinacy made him go to considerable lengths to avoid even listening to music on a friend's radiogram. He turned his back on the past. Too late for him, now, to be a professional pianist, even had two of his fingers not been broken. But he was an artist, and he insisted on severing himself from his roots.

He had lived with despair for ten years, and now he had no intention of relinquishing it. Life, he had seen for himself, was not only brutal, cruel, filthy, but also meaningless. An exercise in futility, as he was fond of saying. One might as well be dead. Or, to be accurate, one had far better be dead.

But his will to live was strong, his whole organism fought for existence at any price. So he came out of the camp, and found himself in London, supported by one of the relief organisations. Because he discovered that life could have some meaning in terms of service to those who had not only had the misfortune to be born into the human race but like him were suffering for it, he turned to medicine. Since he had no means and needed to work, he became a nurse. He passed the state examinations, his English by now fluent.

He had been a staff nurse at the Central London Hospital, and Meg a newly-appointed junior sister, when they had first gone out together. Meg had been strongly attracted to the Austrian Jew with the ugly

gnomish face and figure, who had sur-
mounted so much. He seemed to her to be
immeasurably more mature than the young
men she had previously met. He was witty,
caustic and bitter, and very entertaining
when he chose. His survival against odds
was important to Meg, who longed to
restore happiness to him.

Andy thought it was an excellent joke to
play around with the pretty conventional
sister of such impeccably dull background.
When he married her, it was for what he
could get out of her. If she wanted to put
him through medical school while she
worked – let her. Life owed him that. If she
was hurt in the process, that was her look-
out. She had had it easy so far. Let her find
out that life was not for the soft.

Once he was dependent on her for finan-
cial support, he loathed it. He resented the
part she played in his scheme of life, he
disliked her safe middle-class background,
he detested the fact that she continued to
work, though it was this that enabled him to
study. But in all their quarrels, which were
many, he never went too far, because he
intended to finish his training.

He hated her. He hated her for what she
had given him, and because she was alive,

and blooming (Meg remained a gay crea-
ture, full of colour and life, her dark hair
shining, her eyes clear and full of warmth,
no matter how tired she knew herself to be).
For all his hate, though, he could not have
left her. Because by now he loved her too.
Loved her for the comfort she had brought
him, for the certain loyalty she showed him
over the years, the sure devotion he knew he
could find at home. By now he could not do
without her. So he remained dependent on
her, though he had passed all his examinations, done his house jobs. He had
intended to leave her when she had served
his purpose. This was to be his vengeance
on life, his turning of the tables. But when it
came to it, he couldn't go. Because of this,
he hated her more than ever.

Tonight, however, he was in one of his
infrequent good moods. The party had been
successful, he was pleased with the new
house, pleased with the impression it had
created, pleased that the Ramsays had been
present.

The four of them – Meg and Andy, Michael
and Anne – sat down in the middle of Meg's
cluttered kitchen, modern as a magazine sup-
plement, but in its muddle hardly different
from any old glory hole, to excellent roast

beef. Andy opened a bottle of burgundy, although they all protested they had drunk enough.

'I want it, if you don't,' he said firmly. Mellowed by drink and success, his freakish vitality was overwhelming. It was possible, for once, Anne thought, to have some idea why Meg had married him.

The telephone broke into their enjoyment. Andy went to answer it, came back pleased. 'For you,' he said gleefully to Michael. Andy always rejoiced in the discomfiture of others. 'It's Wooldridge. He says he's worried about the child in the side ward.'

Michael went off to talk to Derek Wooldridge, his registrar. When he came back to the table they broke off their conversation. 'Well?' Meg asked.

'I said I'd go in on my way back – in about half an hour.'

'At least you can finish your meal,' Meg said in satisfied tones.

But Anne felt a pang of bitter disappointment. She had expected to spend the remainder of the evening with Michael, and had looked forward to being driven home by him.

'You'll stay, won't you, Anne?' Meg asked.

'Of course, I'd love to,' Ann said through

her disappointment, instinctively, as was customary with her, hiding her true feelings. In any case, she reminded herself, it would do her little good to accompany Michael. He had already switched off his personal interests and was spiritually back in the wards, although his physical presence cut up ripe Camembert and smeared it over biscuits.

'Andy,' he remarked suddenly, cutting obliviously across their conversation, 'did I hear Uncle Alec was using the new steroid that IDH want us to try out?'

'We have some, yes,' Andy agreed cautiously. He was Ramsay's registrar. 'Not very much. We used it on that case...' he went into detail. 'Just as one would expect,' he ended, 'the cure a good deal worse than the disease.'

'Yes, well, you'd expect a good many side effects. But as a last resort–'

'Oh, as a last resort, yes. I suppose one might then manage to produce some sort of temporary balance–'

'Exactly. And as she's resistant to most of the...'

'Honestly, we might just as well not *exist*,' Meg complained to Anne. This was to put Anne's own thoughts into words, and if possible increased her depression. 'At least I've fed them,' Meg went on, this being her own main preoccupation. 'It's obvious they're both going to spend the next few hours down at the Central, trying out this horrible drug on this poor little poppet, and leaving you and me to clear up here. Do you suppose it could be a put-up job?'

But they both knew it wasn't.

'Anyway,' Meg added, 'we've got the Dishmaster, thank God.'

All very well for her, Anne thought. Andy was probably better out of the house now. No time for reaction to set in, for him to turn suddenly on Meg with one of his scathing, demoralising bursts of venom.

But for herself, Anne experienced a familiar frustrated sense of loss. It was always like this. When she and Michael were getting somewhere, he was called away to a case. The next time she saw him, they would be back at the beginning again, as if they had never walked along this road at all. Yet they had. They were always setting out together along a pathway of hope. Always setting out, and continually interrupted by the demands of hospital, practice, friends, relations. And now, she remembered bitterly, now Jennifer Ramsay was on night duty. Anne was startled to find herself racked with tearing jealousy. Which ward was Jennifer on? She was determined not to ask. She pushed her fear away angrily, and began to load Meg's splendid new washing-up machine.

For the sake of something to say, she asked idly, 'I wonder if someone took Clare home?'

Clare Nicolson was her young secretary, an attractive girl of twenty-two, a hard worker and intelligent. Anne had become very fond of her during the three years they had worked together, and it had been at her prompting that Meg had invited Clare to the house-warming.

'Oh yes,' Meg said at once. 'She left with Dr Onajianya.' He was a Nygandan doctor, highly regarded at the Central.

'Oh,' Anne said, on a downward inflection.

'Surely you don't disapprove?' Meg demanded at once. 'Andy *would* be shocked. He's always saying the English have a terrific colour bar, whatever they may pretend.'

'It's nothing to do with colour,' Anne protested. 'It's simply that Clare's very young still. I hope she won't start going around with Dr Onajianya. I don't think it would be a good idea for her to be involved in anything so – so–' she hesitated, fumbling for words. 'So unorthodox – you can't deny it's that, can you? And difficult. No. In fact I don't think I ought to let her.'

'To *let* her? Who are *you,* by the way? President de Gaulle, or what?'

'I know it sounds silly.'

'Onajianya is a very nice chap,' Meg went on, 'as well as being outstanding as a physician, and I can't see why Clare shouldn't go out with him if she gets the chance, and lucky to have the opportunity. When he goes home to Nyganda he'll be a great man.'

'Yes, but…'

'What would you have said to anyone who thought they had a duty to pick your boy friends at that age?'

'I know. All the same, I do feel responsible, and I don't like it.'

Anne walked away with a tray of glasses and began putting them in a cupboard, feeling on edge, half in the right and half hopelessly in the wrong.

'Let her go to hell in her own way, dear,' Meg shouted from the kitchen, 'same as I did.'

This was the moment of truth, Anne recognised afterwards, when she should have said, 'Meg, how *is* your marriage? What about Andy? Are you glad or sorry?' And Meg would have told her, was probably longing to tell her. But Anne had dodged it. She couldn't get the words out.

For Meg, too, the moment passed. She was thankful she hadn't spilt the beans, as for a fleeting few minutes she had longed to do.

They both began talking about the guests, having a comfortable post-party comparing of notes – Lady Ramsay's hat, honestly, where *does* she get them? – Miss Glossop's infuriating and immovable stance by the door – Jennifer's astonishing good looks, must be some genetic freak – Derek Woold-ridge's girl friend, did you *see* her dress, my dear, they were all so anatomical about it, they are impossible, they said down to...

'Look, Anne, why don't you stay the night?' Meg suggested. 'We've got our new spare room – do say you will?'

Anne accepted, and Meg took her upstairs to give her towels and nightdress and to make up the bed. She was in the bathroom when Andy came back and shouted for Meg.

He and Michael had both returned. Michael had come to fetch Anne.

'Oh, you can't, Michael, she's staying here for the night. Anne, come down and talk to Michael, he's come all the way back to fetch you.'

Anne, flushed and disturbed, her hair loose on her shoulders, came barefoot down the stairs, still pink from the bath, in a flimsy nightdress and Meg's sprigged housecoat. Michael, hovering on the edge of desire, was for once swept off his feet. They talked unsatisfactorily while Meg made tea and Andy put the car away. Meg came in with the tea, Andy and Michael discussed the treatment of the child they had been seeing, they all talked about the party – Lady Ramsay's *hat*, Derek's girl friend...

Eventually Michael left for the second time, and Anne went to bed in a state of pleasant agitation. Michael had come back for her – why had she accepted Meg's invitation to stay, why had no warning bell rung in her head? Yet still she bubbled with joy and anticipation. She knew she had been right. This evening had been the same for them both, they were in love, and tomorrow would have meaning again.

Michael meanwhile drove down from Hampstead back to his Wimpole Street flat, on edge with frustrated desire. Suddenly he remembered Jennifer on night duty. He could at least talk to her for a bit – useless to think of going back to the flat to sleep. He parked the car and went to the wards.

The following Monday morning Anne was in her office talking to Clare about one of the Nygandan nurses whom Miss Glossop had had to discipline. Anne had returned to her own room after defending him, though her sympathies had been on the other side. 'He was nearly sent packing this time,' she commented. 'Matron had about had enough. I can't say I'm surprised, either.'

'It might not have been such a bad idea. He could have gone back to Ikerobe with Kezia,' Clare remarked casually, looking up from her typewriter.

'Kezia?'

'She's his girl friend. You know, she was the staff nurse on Jenner. That's what's the matter with him, of course. I expect he'll be all right once she's finally gone and he settles down again.'

'Doesn't he want her to go back, then?'

'No, he wants her to stay, and then they can both go on nursing here and get all sorts of certificates and things.'

Anne wondered if Clare had heard all this from Onajianya. Were they going about together? And what business was it of hers if they were? Ought she to say anything to Clare?

She would ask Michael what he thought,

she decided. Perhaps he would agree with Meg, and see nothing wrong in their friendship. After all, Onajianya had been his house physician. He knew him well, knew what sort of man he was. Yes, she would discuss it with Michael.

Today she was happy. No problem really worried her. At last she and Michael were ready to move forward into a new relationship together. She had felt this on Saturday night, and she had been right. He must have felt it also, to have driven back to Hampstead for her. True, he had not rung her on Sunday, as she had hoped he would. But that meant nothing.

The day went by, and she heard nothing from him, nor, as it turned out, did she meet him anywhere about the hospital. She was disappointed, but unworried. He would ring her in the evening. She knew, now, that the certainty between them was mutual. He was having a busy day, no doubt, might even have had to go out of London to see a patient. A day or two was of no importance.

But the days went by.

Soon she met him one morning in the corridor outside her room, another afternoon in the library, one evening in the pub they all frequented. He was friendly enough, there was no stiffness between them. But there was *nothing* between them.

It was the old story.

Anne went through her pattern of emotions. She already knew them well, yet repetition could not armour her against them. Michael had been responsible for this unhappiness before, more than once – would she never learn, she asked herself furiously? But she had to live through it all again, slowly, day by day, agonisingly. Disbelief, questioning, heart-searching, anger, disbelief again. Hope that refused to die. Sorrow and a childish sense of loss. Then emptiness and desolation. At last this was followed in its turn, but unusually, by a feeling of irritation, of impatience. She was tired of Michael Vanstone. She would not be bothered with him any longer. Enough was enough.

A comforting sensation of renewed pleasure in day to day activities came to her then, an enjoyment of cups of coffee, of chat, of beer in the pub in the evening, of knitting tranquilly, at home in the dusk, a busy day safely behind, another to follow. She began to enjoy her own flat again. She had lived in it with Tim. It had been bought for them by her father, for she and Tim had been far too insolvent to have lived in anything but the cheapest of bed-sitting-rooms. But Murray Colegate had not only bought the flat, but had given Anne the furniture that had been in store since her mother's death. The result was that Anne's flat belonged a little to a previous generation. The furniture consisted of antique pieces of some value that had been in her mother's family, and comfortable sofas and chairs from Maples. It was all a little reminiscent of the best waiting-rooms in Harley Street. During Tim's life this had merely been a background for rugger scarves, textbooks, bones, specimen jars, slides, gramophone records, crampons, ice axes, ropes, rucksacks, maps, cameras and bottles of beer. But Anne was naturally tidy, and the vivid cluttered past had long been hidden away in cupboards.

The flat was Anne's refuge and over the years she had grown very fond of it, with its spacious rooms and its air of subdued calm and stability. While she had been filled with thoughts of Michael, she had allowed it to become dusty, a little neglected. Now she filled vases with spring flowers, first with tulips and forsythia, then, as the months went by, with lilac and the first roses. She led a satisfying and undisturbed life, if empty.

When Meg invited her to stay in the new

Hampstead house with her while Andy was on tour in Nyganda for three weeks, she accepted with alacrity. But she did not confide in her the story of her recent disappointment. She and Meg had been at school together, and the theory was that they told one another everything. In practice they discussed recipes, clothes, make-up, exchanged hospital gossip – and little else. Anne had always been self-contained, almost secretive, but in the past Meg had been open. She had discussed her deepest feelings almost as they occurred. But when she had married Andy everything had changed.

Now at last Meg was beginning to discover her own hidden feelings about Andy, which until recently she had refused to admit even to herself, let alone to Anne. Until he was established and successful, he had remained her mission, no matter how he behaved. She had been determined to give him what life owed him, to make up to him for all his years of misery. But now everything had been achieved, even to the dream house and her own possession of leisure, she was unable to conceal any longer her increasing dislike of him. The years of deception were over. She lay alone in bed in the new house, and rejoiced in his absence on tour in Africa. Understood, with shock and horror, but clarity, that she was dreading his return.

When she had invited Anne to stay she had intended to confide in her at last, to tell her of her depression and her disillusion. But she had not, when it came to the point, been able to do this. To speak of her un-happiness would somehow make it final, irrevocable.

What she had done, with a purpose that was hardly clear to herself, was to invite Miss Glossop to dinner while Andy (who would have objected to her presence at his table) was safely out of the country.

Meg and Anne were waiting for her, sitting, on this warm June evening, outside in the patio, gay with petunias spilling from painted tubs, purple clematis climbing to-wards the pergola, from which hung baskets trailing pink geraniums. Above them, the sky was blue and birds talked in the high Hampstead trees... It was no wonder, Anne thought, that Meg, after all the years of overwork and stuffy London lodgings, should glory in all this. At the same time she poked fun at her newly-attained retreat.

'All we need is a flood-lamp and a fountain, and we'd be ready for the models and the photographer from *Vogue*,' she remarked sarcastically. 'All the same,' she added honestly, 'I must say it's tremendously pleasant to be able to lie in the sun here, instead of paying threepence for a deck-chair in Russell Square.' She stretched, and drank gin and tonic. 'Surely there must be a new story about somebody?' she asked next.

Anne considered. 'Well, there's the new name for Dr Goldsmith – the obstetrician, not the anaesthetist, I mean.'

'What do they call him?' Meg asked lazily.

'Goldfinger.'

They were both laughing weakly when the gate clicked open and Miss Glossop joined them. A big, stately woman, the Hon. Beryl Glossop looked elderly already, with grey hair, worn features and a ruddy complexion. Her appearance, her manner, and her clothes set her firmly in the fifties, though she was as it happened still in her middle forties. She was fond of Meg, who had been one of her ward sisters for nearly ten years. She knew how hard Meg had worked to run her marriage and her ward. She did not, perhaps, know a great deal about marriage, but she knew exactly what effort went into a well-run ward, and she knew how tiresome

Andy Taussig could be as a doctor. She did not suppose he was any less tiresome as a husband.

She accepted a drink, commented favourably on the house. 'Enjoying your leisure, sister?' she then asked briskly. She waited for no answer. The query had been more of a statement of fact – you'd better be, she meant, or else back on the wards and pull your weight. 'I wonder how Dr Taussig and Dr Vanstone are getting on in Nyganda? Anyway, one thing we know, they'll get plenty of work there.'

'I should think they'd be at it from morning to night,' Meg agreed. 'Fortunately Andy never minds the heat.'

'I hope Dr Vanstone will be able to stand up to it,' Miss Glossop said gloomily. 'Now there's a young man who's going far,' she added, brightening.

Anne stiffened. She and Meg had laid bets as to how long it would before they were told of someone 'going far'. One of Miss Glossop's favourite conjectures. Anne would have preferred to have lost her bet, rather than to have Michael brought into such a discussion.

'Michael Vanstone has always been exceptionally able,' Meg was remarking, hoping, evidently, to encourage Miss Glossop to further flights of oratory in her well-known style.

'*Professor* Vanstone before next year is out,' she rejoined meaningly, her sturdy legs in their stretch nylon stockings comfortably extended on the long chair, waving her glass of gin dangerously.

'Do you think so?' Meg asked, interested now. 'It might be Bill Barham, surely, or...' she mentioned two other men, older than Vanstone, who might be expected to have the Chair of Medicine when Sir Alexander Ramsay, known to the entire hospital as Uncle Alec, retired the following summer.

'What Uncle Alec says will carry a great deal of weight,' Miss Glossop pointed out. 'And I don't for a minute think it's accidental that he's sent Dr Vanstone to Nyganda this year instead of going himself.'

'I thought it might be just that the old boy thought the heat and the pace might be too much for him. After all, he did have that coronary last year.'

'But why Dr *Vanstone* instead?' Miss Glossop enquired portentously. 'Oh no, there's more to it than that, sister. Everyone's talking about it. Uncle Alec's made his choice, they say, and he's grooming Dr Vanstone.'

She paused, and her free hand, unknown to her, performed the motions of grooming a horse.

'They've been saying that for years,' Meg retorted with truth. 'Ever since Michael was his house physician. Surely he should be well and truly groomed by now?'

Miss Glossop disregarded this. 'And then,' she continued, 'what about young Jennifer Ramsay, eh?'

'What about Jennifer Ramsay, then?' Meg asked, now at a loss. Anne had not passed on this bit of hospital gossip to her.

'Good gracious, sister, haven't you heard?' Miss Glossop asked irritably, in the tone she would have used if Meg had been belated in discovering some arrangement that affected her ward routine. 'I should have thought–' she recollected Anne's part in the talk, and realised why Meg had not heard of this from her. She hesitated for a moment, then, typically, decided to plunge. Mrs Heseltine would have to hear the talk sooner or later. She had better learn, Beryl Glossop thought in her usual arbitrary fashion, to put a good face on the situation, and she might as well begin here and now.

Anne saw what was coming, flinched, and drank the last of her gin.

'*Everyone,*' Miss Glossop was declaiming, 'is expecting her to announce her engagement to Dr Vanstone at any *moment.*'

'Good lord,' Meg said, shaken. 'But – but she – she's so young.' This was the only impediment she was able to produce, with Anne sitting there looking icily distant.

'Got her head screwed on,' Miss Glossop retorted, as though this were the first requirement. 'And it would be extremely suitable. Though I must say I think she's a very lucky girl. She'll take her finals next year, and then I suppose they'll marry, and Dr Vanstone will have the Chair.'

'Lucky Michael, I should say,' Meg remarked.

'Oh well, he deserves success, if anyone does,' Miss Glossop responded with certainty. Hardworking, polite, and never wild, she meant. 'He has extremely good judgement,' she added.

'And a sense of timing,' Meg pointed out with acerbity. She was well aware of Anne's love for Michael, and had herself thought them to be at last on the edge of an affair. She could see, though, that Jennifer Ramsay was what her mother would call 'a better catch', and she felt correspondingly angry with Michael on Anne's behalf. She could easily, with the practice of twenty years, read Anne's deliberately blank expression, and knew she was finding the conversation painful.

She had intended to pour another round of gin and tonic, but instead made a move indoors to dinner, and chattered volubly while settling them at the vast teak table and serving, first, the chilled melon, then the cold salmon and salad, and pouring the hock. Anne abetted her – as well she might, Meg thought with irritable affection. Why had she confided nothing of all this? – and praised the salmon, the green salad, the potato mayonnaise with chives, the French dressing ('my new mixer – no trouble at all,' Meg explained). Miss Glossop, who enjoyed her food, was happily diverted, drank the hock and smacked her lips, and began to tell an involved story about a difficult nurse. Meg refilled her glass. 'M-mm?' she queried absently, 'staff trouble?'

'My dear, when isn't there staff trouble?' Miss Glossop asked bracingly. 'I expect it. It never disturbs me. I never allow it to. But there is more trouble than usual at present.' She drank again, stared like a broody hen out of the immense window that filled one wall of the room.

'So Anne said,' Meg agreed. 'New lot not settling?'

'No, they aren't. There's something wrong with them.' She stared challengingly at Anne.

'Do you really think so?' she asked placatingly.

'My dear girl, you know it as well as I do,' Miss Glossop boomed.

The trouble was, Anne did. Her office had been besieged for months with sisters, charge nurses, doctors, complaining or warning her about the behaviour of one or other of the Nygandan students. Then there were the Nygandans themselves, constantly telling her how difficult life was, and how no one at the Central (except, they hoped, herself) understood their problems.

She sighed. 'They do seem to be an unusually temperamental lot this year,' she admitted unwillingly.

'You've said it,' Miss Glossop cried in a fake American accent. They were well into the second bottle of hock now. 'What I want to know,' she rapped out, banging Anne uncomfortably in the chest, 'is, what is all this talk of bribes, eh? Tell me that, young woman.'

'I wish I knew,' Anne said uncomfortably.

'Do you think it can be true?'

'There's some reason why this year's intake is so much below our usual standard, and I see no sense in refusing to admit that the cause may well be money. What I want to know is, what can Dr Barham have been thinking of? Anyway, it's cooked his goose.'

'He can't have known anything about it,' Ann protested. 'Besides, he's the dean of the medical school. The nurses' selection–'

'Oh, I know he's a friend of yours,' Miss Glossop interrupted accusingly. She gave the impression that not only was this a deliberate move on Anne's part, entirely designed to annoy, but that it invalidated anything she might have to say on the subject. 'It's no good shutting your eyes to reality. He's out there, he's the senior medical man, and if he doesn't know what's going on he ought to. After all, he's the dean, isn't he?' She paused infinitesimally, then, evidently recollecting what Anne had said about the medical school, rushed on. 'Anyway, as I said, he's cooked his goose as far as getting the Chair's concerned. He ought to know better.'

Bill Barham had been Tim Heseltine's chief. Tim had admired him. He had also been infuriated by him, as people often were. A big jovial man, who radiated energy and brimmed over with zestful confidence, Bill was impulsive. Always busy, immersed in a hundred plans, his different objectives were often incompatible with one another. This would be obvious to others, but very seldom to Bill, who was eternally optimistic. He cared about people. He would move mountains to help them out of holes they had fallen into as the result of what others could see clearly was their own stupidity. Sometimes his help was unwise, as the onlookers saw. But he was warmhearted and he seldom stopped to think. He acted. Many cursed him. Many unlikely people were devoted to him. He inspired love and fury, in about equal proportions.

When Tim Heseltine had been killed climbing in the Dolomites, it had been Bill Barham who had taken the next plane, leaving his appointments, clinics, ward rounds and lectures in confusion. Anne still remembered the feeling of comfort that the mere sight of his burly figure had brought her in her shocked misery. Square-jawed, heavy-browed, with a snub nose and close-cropped black hair that curled like a lamb's fleece despite all his efforts to prevent it, Bill looked – and was – immensely capable. His patients trusted him to look after them, and Anne had the same faith. It had been Bill who had seen to everything, who had brought Anne home, who had found her the post as Secretary to the Nyganda Foundation at the Central London Hospital and insisted on her taking it.

Now Bill was in Nyganda. And the new intake of nursing students were unsatisfactory – the worst the Central had known for years – and there was this talk of bribes. The trouble was that lately, like so many of them at the Central, he had been overworked and understaffed. Anne could guess what had happened. Bill would have so many projects in action that it would never have crossed his mind to ensure adequate supervision of the nurses' selection. But he should have seen to it. As Miss Glossop said, a failure in Nyganda was going to harm him.

For Bill was one of those in line, with Michael Vanstone, for the Chair of Medicine at the Central London Medical School. Bill wanted the Chair, Anne knew that, wanted it badly. But if he had failed, had slipped ever so slightly, during his year in Nyganda, Uncle Alec would never back him. This was what they were all saying, and

Anne knew they were right.

Sir Alexander Ramsay had his own loyalties, and one of the strongest was to the Nyganda Foundation. He had initiated it, sponsored it, guided it through its early years, and remained its Chairman still. His father had been a district officer in Nyganda in the old colonial days, and his childhood and youth were bound up in the country. He had its future very much at heart, and he watched the young men from the Central closely to see how they made out during their tours of service there. Ramsay regarded the period in Nyganda as a testing time for younger colleagues, a period designed to show up a man's innate qualities. No longer buttressed by staff of all grades and types, laboratory services, specialists to turn to, he had to make out on his own. Brilliance was not enough, common sense, stability, improvisation – all these were required. If a man lacked some vital quality, a year in Nyganda would demonstrate this. At any rate, Uncle Alec thought so.

'I know Dr Barham's a friend of yours,' Miss Glossop was infuriatingly repeating. 'But he ought to be more careful. Not that I mind, of course. In fact, I'm rather pleased. What's happened suits me down to the ground. It proves my point. It's only what I've been saying all along. Now they'll have to listen to me, for a change. I've always said we should only bring trained nurses over here from Nyganda. The present system's too much for all but the cream of them.'

'I'm sure it'd be too much for me,' Meg agreed. 'When I think of what they take on, it staggers me. I couldn't have done it.'

'Of course, sister. We expect far too much. At the next nursing committee I shall bring it up again. With this year's intake as an example of what can happen if we aren't perpetually on our toes–' unconsciously she pointed to her own toes under the table, and hit her knee with a resounding thwack on the teak top as a result. She looked startled, and began massage. '–I think we may get our training school out in Nyganda at last. I've always wanted one there, as I've told you before, sister. But you know what these wretched doctors are – they want all the available money for research, and think they can staff the hospital on the cheap, as usual.' She paused, then added, 'What I shall need then, of course, is a good young matron to run the training school. Go-ahead, flexible, but capable of maintaining Central nursing standards.' She pursed her lips over the final three words, which were frequently on her lips. Then she sighed. 'All my best sisters get married. Look at you, sister.' Meg obediently tried to give the impression that she was achieving this unlikely feat. 'Look at young Jennifer Ramsay.' Meg switched her gaze to the window, as though Jennifer were to be seen floating outside. Then she looked amazed. 'She'll take her finals next year,' Matron was announcing, when Meg's surprise evidently penetrated. 'No, no,' she said irritably, 'I know she won't be nearly ready to take a matron's post then. But in another six or seven years, a post in Nyganda, running our training school, would be just the thing for a capable young gel like her. But there won't be a chance. She'll be well and truly married to Dr Vanstone by then, raising a family. By the time her children have grown up her nursing will be completely out of date, and she'll have forgotten how to be *disciplined*.' She turned down her mouth at this total demoralisation, while Meg concealed a grin. 'In any case,' she went on, 'she'll never learn how to run a ward, I don't suppose I'll even have her as a staff nurse. Her training will be completely *wasted*.'

'What a pity,' Meg said in honeyed tones.

Miss Glossop was not fooled. 'You're

laughing at me, sister,' she said loudly. 'And you think I don't know why. You're wrong. But my job is to train staff to run this hospital, not to act as a marriage bureau.'

Anne gave a surprised glance round Meg's attractive living-room with the curtains from Edinburgh Weavers, the trough of plants, the Swan chairs by Arne Jacobsen and the long low coffee table. She almost expected it to have changed without her knowledge into a ward at the Central.

'You may think it's a better life for Jennifer Ramsay to marry Dr Vanstone. I simply see a good potential sister wasted. Now, *you're* being wasted. What are *you* doing playing about pretending to run this house all day long? Eh?'

Meg opened her mouth.

'Why don't you get a housekeeper?'

'I – I don't think–'

'You needn't tell me,' Miss Glossop interrupted. 'I know. Dr Taussig wouldn't *like* it. What business has he got to like it? Tell me that. Eh? Suppose you took it into your head that you'd like him to do all the gardening, so that you could come home to beautiful lawns and a profusion of flowers after your hospital day? Would he take the slightest notice? Of course he wouldn't. But he says

45

the same sort of thing to you, and you give up nursing. Women. They're all the same. They must be for ever pleasing some man. Why can't they do a straightforward job of work, and fit the rest of their lives round it?'

Meg had been vibrating with suppressed laughter, and began now to hoot helplessly.

'That's right, don't take me seriously,' Miss Glossop said, affronted. 'I'm right, though. All my best nurses get married and leave. My only hope is that they marry thoroughly unsatisfactorily, and then I can at least keep them for some years.'

As this final remark applied exactly to Meg, both she and Anne were silenced, while Miss Glossop glared triumphantly.

Shortly afterwards she left, and Meg at once turned on Anne.

'What's all this about Michael and Jennifer?' she demanded. 'Why haven't you told me about it? What's been happening? I didn't even know they were going around together, let alone on the point of getting engaged, as Matron seems to think. What an old gossip-monger she is.'

'It's hospital talk,' Anne said. 'I don't know.'

'I thought *you* were going around with him?'

'So did I. In a way.'

'There's only one way, dear.'

'Well, I mean – he – I–'

'Has he said anything to you?'

'About Jennifer?'

'No, you nit. About you and him.'

'Not exactly,' Anne hedged.

'What do you mean, "not exactly"?' Meg asked crossly. 'Are you in MI5 or something? Give.'

'I suppose I mean he's never said anything actually specific.' Anne was annoyed to find herself blushing. The trouble was, whenever she examined what Michael had said to her, it amounted to less than it had seemed to mean when they were together, when it had been accompanied by long looks and meaningful silences. When it came down to it, what had he said, beyond suggesting that she looked particularly attractive, or that she was unusually understanding? 'I've often thought he was on the verge of committing himself, but I don't suppose he ever actually has,' she said unhappily. 'He always leaves you to read between the lines.' She smiled waveringly.

Meg was amazed. 'Do you mean to say – Andy and I both thought – are you honestly telling me – I was sure–'

'So was I,' Anne said in a rush, suddenly finding herself able to push out the committing words, and once she had begun, unable to stop. 'I was, too. I have thought for some time, and – and on and off I've been quite worked up about it.'

'Me too,' Meg interjected.

Anne stared at her, startled. The situation was certainly not a figment of her imagination, if Meg knew about it.

'Andy always said it wouldn't do,' Meg added casually.

Anne was immediately indignant. 'Why on earth not?' she demanded.

Meg grinned. 'He said you'd be too much for Michael,' she said. 'He thinks Michael is a cold fish.'

Anne was furious.

Chapter 2

As soon as Andy Taussig returned from Nyganda, he and Meg gave another party. Anne went to Hampstead to help with the preparations. Soon after lunch, she was in the kitchen, making cheese dip, filling pastry cases, cutting olives and gherkins, spreading biscuits, pricking sausages, polishing glasses, arranging flowers. She was still there when the first guests arrived, and went up to change only when Meg and Andy were already talking to half a dozen early arrivals.

The day had been hot, and the cool of the evening was welcome. Anne had a quick shower in the bathroom adjoining the spare room, and changed into a loose silk shift of that season's *art nouveau* greens and blues. Relaxed, but hardly interested in the party – no high hopes this time, she thought, none of that sentimental nonsense – she sauntered downstairs and was at once pounced on by Miss Glossop, posted once again at the living-room door.

'Now, Mrs Heseltine, I was wondering

where *you* could have got to?' she cried, all but poking Anne in the midriff, and waving her glass wildly. She laughed – or, rather, neighed like a horse. However, there was hardly a soul at the party who was not from the Central, and no one took any notice of the strange sound, quite usual to them. She repeated her remark, 'Yes, I was wondering where *you* could have got to. Because we all know,' she broadcast firmly, 'what *great* friends you and sister are, so I knew you must be somewhere about.' She looked arch. 'Because I've been waiting to have a little talk with you,' she ended ominously.

'Oh,' Anne said weakly. 'Yes?'

'About the Nyganda training school. Now you and I must get together over this, or these doctors will be too much for us. They'll take all the money for research if we aren't careful, you know.'

Anne blinked. She had always been able to get along reasonably well with Miss Glossop, but this you and I together was entirely new. She tried not to sigh. The party was going to be even drearier than she had feared. She grinned to herself. What are you beefing about, she thought sarcastically? Isn't everyone agreed that this is what parties are for, to advance careers, initiate new alignments? You are out of the romantic twenties, my girl, when parties were for starting love affairs, and into the planning, lobbying, campaigning thirties.

'...at the next committee in September, you see. So I wanted to be sure before then...'

Anne pulled herself together. She really must listen to what Miss Glossop was saying. Apart from anything else, it would be awkward, to say the least, when she came to prepare the papers for the meeting, if she had no idea what all this was about.

'...the Chairman on our side.'

Our side?

'But a good deal depends on having the item fairly high on the agenda.'

Blow me, Anne thought. Can all this simply be that she wants the training school placed high on the agenda?'

She had forgotten to allow for the influence of alcohol. Beryl Glossop had come to the party with the intention of lobbying Anne in any case, but her naturally boisterous personality had been warmed by Andy's whisky. In addition, while in theory she approved of the romance between Michael Vanstone and Jennifer Ramsay, in practice she was sorry for Anne, widowed once and now, she feared, abandoned by Michael for the young girl. She felt nearer to Anne than she had done before. There had been a time – twenty years ago now – when Beryl Glossop, a handsome girl with a glowing face and a too-hearty laugh, had gone out with Jimmy Marlow, the heart surgeon, then a young casualty officer. It had never led anywhere, he had dropped her and eventually he married a young slip of a thing from the almoner's office, but she had always retained a special affection for him. Now she saw Anne meeting the same experience. Life was dealing hardly with her, but she was standing up to it well. Beryl Glossop considered she had done the same, and she was companionably disposed towards anyone seen treading the same path – though she saw no reason why it should be made any easier than it had been for her. At the moment, in any case, she did genuinely need Anne's support. The plan for the training school in Nyganda, which she had brought up at the Nursing Committee, had been referred to the Nyganda Foundation. The intention had been, as she very well knew, to defer any decision on the project. Any excuse for delay would be taken. If those against the new training school could postpone action on it until after Sir Alexander

Ramsay's retirement next year, they had as good as won. The school was not at all Michael Vanstone's cup of tea. He would want the money for clinical trials. They had all heard him expounding his ideas on this subject. He was doing so now.

'Far too much rushing about starting ploys which we haven't the staff or the equipment to complete adequately,' he was telling a group who had gathered round to hear his stories of the recent visit. Michael had had a good deal to drink by this time, he was comfortably at home in Andy's house, and he was much less guarded than usual in his remarks. 'It's *useless,* in my opinion, to go dashing about here, there and everywhere, into every bush village, up the river, into the hills, down into the swamps, outpatients here, surgery there, dosing children with any old drug you happen to have left, knowing it can't do harm and may well do good, delivering pregnant women in the backs of Land-Rovers – Barham, I think, confidently expects one to perform an appendicectomy with a pen-knife up a tree if required.' He paused, and there was an obedient ripple of laughter, led by Derek Wooldridge. 'That is no way to use senior physicians and surgeons,' he continued. 'We can't do everything that needs doing – we couldn't do more than make a beginning if we went so far as to transplant the entire Central, lock, stock and barrel, to Nyganda for five years. It's useless, pointless, to wear ourselves out pretending we can. We have to choose a limited field and act in it competently and where our example will be of some value. Not rush about like demented Victorian missionaries, turning our hands to whatever comes up. Bill seems quite prepared to do just that. I'm not only not prepared to do it myself, I think it's emphatically the wrong policy. Entirely the wrong policy. Uneconomic, unsound. Thoroughly unsound.'

There was a murmur. At the Central, to label a policy or a man unsound was to damn him for ever. It was no secret that Michael Vanstone considered Bill Barham unsound, but for him to say so publicly, before Uncle Alec too, was startling. More than one of those present saw that the battle for the Chair of Medicine had passed the preliminary stage of diplomatic skirmishing. It was now clearly joined.

'As I see it,' Michael was saying, 'the whole untouched field is far too vast for us to attempt. We must till a small corner as an example. In fact, what we must do is *teach*.

That's our job. We should do some teaching clinics. We can't attempt to handle the colossal hordes who besiege the rural clinics, and it's useless to try, as I've told Bill. It's nothing but a confidence trick to pretend we can.'

The audience stirred again. Michael had once, in an unguarded moment, referred to Barham as the 'confidence trickster'. Though he was unaware of the impact of the phrase, no one had forgotten it.

'We should stay in the few main centres, where there are at least staff and facilities for reasonable work. Then, apart from teaching, what I want to see started is properly-controlled clinical trials. There we have virgin territory. Now, my idea is…' he went off into a detailed discussion of drug dosages, resistant organisms, advanced disease, control groups, statistical methods. They all became involved in argument.

Uncle Alec left them, and wandered out into Meg's patio, a thoughtful expression on his face, sad, humorous, gentle, a little sardonic.

Miss Glossop, like a friendly but urgent child, tugged Anne's arm. 'Come along,' she said. 'Come along. Now's our chance.'

Anne reluctantly accompanied her to

where Ramsay was puffing his pipe under the pergola, Meg's hanging baskets trailing ivy, tradescantia and pink geraniums above his smoke-rings.

'Well, Matron?' he said jovially.

'I'm thinking about my training school,' Miss Glossop said implacably.

Anne thought Uncle Alec looked tired. He was getting old, and he had had enough, she suspected, of clinical trials and nurse training schools, and would have liked to enjoy his pipe in peace. A year or two ago they had all been saying it was impossible to imagine that he would ever accept retirement, he was so full of drive and vigour. Then he had had his coronary. He had made a wonderful recovery, and apart from the fact that he had succeeded in losing over a stone in weight, he had seemed unchanged. Just lately, though, he had been perceptibly ageing, Anne had the impression now that he might even be looking forward to the quiet of his retirement.

At this moment Meg, as though conjured up by Anne's thought, appeared and bore Miss Glossop away. 'Now Matron,' she said in her most managing voice, 'I haven't had a chance to talk to you all evening. I wanted to ask you...' They disappeared into the house, to be replaced by Derek Wooldridge, also doing his duty.

'Anne, let me get you another drink – where's your glass?'

'Somewhere about, I seem to have lost it,' she said vaguely. In fact, this being one of the penalties of being a friend of the family, no one until now had offered her a drink. Meg and Andy assumed she would forage for herself. But Miss Glossop had given her no time for this. Anne had not tasted the food she and Meg had been preparing all afternoon. Miss Glossop had seen to that, pinning her down at the door. Not even a cheese straw, a potato crisp, or a twiglet had passed her lips. 'No need to hand anything round,' Meg had announced earlier. 'We know these greedy pigs. If we simply put it out on tables here and there, it'll vanish in the first half-hour.' It had.

'Well,' Derek persevered, 'what are you drinking, then? I'll try and find you another glass.'

'Gin,' Anne said hopefully. 'Gin and French.' Nothing like making up for lost time, she thought.

'And you, sir?' This was the reason Wooldridge had come out – to look after the old man.

'Another whisky, m'boy, if you don't mind.'

Derek too disappeared into the house.

Ramsay sighed – a comfortable sigh. 'Let's sit down, m'dear, on these odd looking chairs, and enjoy a bit of peace and quiet, eh? How's y'father?'

'Very well, thank you. He's coming over, you know, in a month or two.'

'Good, good. Look forward to that. Haven't seen him for – must be going on for five or six years.'

'It's six years since he was here last,' Anne agreed.

Ramsay could have kicked himself. Six years ago – that had been when Colegate had flown over after Tim Heseltine's death. Clumsy old fool he was getting. However, no good crying over spilt milk. He settled down for a comfortable talk. He was fond of the daughter of his former pupil, Murray Colegate, and often felt *in loco parentis*. It amused him, too, to see her father in her. The same good looks, the same unexpected touches of formality, reserve.

Derek Wooldridge appeared, with two glasses, which he presented. He sat down firmly on a neighbouring chair, and as soon as the conversation gave him an opening, took it. 'I wonder, sir,' he began, 'if I might show you my paper for the *Lancet?*'

This was the outside of enough. Wooldridge's papers were a tedious and recurrent hazard.

'You may not, m'boy. Another time, another time,' the old man said firmly, and heaved himself to his feet. 'Got to be going now.' He lumbered into the house.

Derek looked disappointed, but decided to make do with Anne as audience. 'Would you like to have a look at it, Anne?' he asked. 'If you could look over the grammar, and so on...' his voice died away, and there in front of her the typescript had materialised. 'Most grateful,' the voice murmured. Wishing she had the moral courage to walk into the house like Uncle Alec, but knowing she lacked it, Anne obediently bent her head.

'This paragraph here,' Derek was saying, 'do you think I've made it sufficiently clear? I was wondering if...' He spent some time telling her what he was wondering, giving various platitudinous alternative versions of an extremely dull paragraph about the method of his investigation. 'Do you think,' he finally demanded, 'I've made it quite clear that each group was selected entirely at random, and that the assessors had no means of knowing to which group each patient had been allocated?'

Anne was bored. 'Don't you think,' she asked devilishly, knowing from experience that this remark never failed to spread alarm, 'that you ought to have had a control group, as well?'

Derek paled. 'Oh,' he said blankly. 'Do you think so? I am only comparing–'

'I know, but can you compare them if you haven't a control group not receiving either dose?'

'Oh.'

'And oughtn't you to take statistical advice – to be on the safe side?'

'Oh,' Derek said again, like a chastened child.

There was silence. He agitatedly ruffled through the pages of his typescript, muttering to himself, and staring frantically at the sky through the pergola while apparently working out fractions. Anne looked at the roses, drooping after the heat of the day, and shedding their petals on the paving. The evening was quiet, most of the guests seemed to have left, and she lay in her chair, overcome by inertia and wondering if Derek would get her another drink, or whether he was so locked on to his paper as to be unaware of all else.

They were joined by Michael Vanstone, to whom Derek immediately put his query about a control group.

'But of course,' Michael said in surprise. 'Do you mean to say you haven't one? The whole investigation's completely invalid without.' His voice, always clipped, was cutting, and Derek flushed.

Michael, disposed of him in a few brief sentences, and Derek escaped indoors, ostensibly to fetch Anne a drink, though she felt it unlikely he would reappear.

'Well now,' Michael said affably, 'don't seem to have seen much of *you*, lately. What have you been up to?'

Oh no, you don't, Anne thought bitterly. 'Don't seem to have seen much of *you*,' indeed. Whose fault was that? One thing was certain, she was not going to make a fool of herself again.

'Why not try looking out for me on the tops of buses occasionally?' she asked caustically.

Michael shot her a startled look.

At this moment Andy came across the side of the patio, seeing off a group of people, including, not only Derek Wooldridge and his girl friend, but also, Anne was irritated to notice, Clare and Onajianya. Clare gave her a friendly wave, and Onajianya his formal bow, before they disappeared through the high gate, and Andy shut it behind them.

'That's the last of them, thank God,' he said loudly, caring nothing for his guests walking along the pavement outside. 'Now we can have supper. Don't move, you two, it's all ready on the trolley, Meg will bring it. We'll clear up inside after we've eaten.'

Meg shortly appeared, wheeling the large teak trolley, and they settled down to eat and chat. 'If I hadn't seen it I wouldn't have believed it,' Meg said. 'I honestly wouldn't. They are all just a lot of greedy schoolboys. It's exactly like feeding the Lower Fourth – except that they know what's expensive and what isn't. Do you know, the smoked salmon and the titchy bit of caviare we had simply got wolfed in the first ten minutes. Late comers go without. Then they liked the Quiche, Anne, that went next. It was good,' she added smugly. 'Didn't you think?'

'Didn't get any. They were too quick for me,' Anne said briefly.

'Oh my *lamb*, how stinking,' Meg commiserated. Andy fidgeted. He hated Meg to behave in what he considered to be an exaggerated English bourgeoise manner. He had educated her out of this, except when she was excited, or had been drinking. He scowled at her now in warning, to make it quite clear that he disapproved.

'I'll make another tomorrow,' Meg promised, ignoring Andy, though a tiny line appeared between her brows, 'and you can come to supper, you and Michael, and eat it – yes?'

Michael accepted immediately. He had tasted the Quiche, he admitted, and would appreciate more of it.

Tonight there was cold chicken, with salad, and then strawberries. Meg began handing the chicken round, while Andy poured the chilled rosé they were to drink. Talk became desultory. Lady Ramsay had not been there (she was in Lucerne, with Jennifer, who had been forced to take her holiday at a time that did not fit in with Uncle Alec's plans) and there was no outrageous hat to discuss. Derek Wooldridge's girl friend had been wearing another low-cut dress, the cleavage on this occasion having been in front instead of at the back, and the depth, they decided, exactly similar.

'Perhaps it's the same dress, back to front,' Meg suggested.

'Derek is becoming boring,' Michael remarked. 'Repetitive. Set in his ways. Same girl friend, same dress, *and* the same tedious paper for publication in the *Lancet*.'

'Surely one of them must have appeared by now?' Andy asked idly, tipping the wine in his glass, and squinting through it at the roses. He had momentarily forgotten his annoyance.

'Oh, I don't think they ever *accept* them,' Michael replied. 'After all, they aren't quite *Lancet* standard, are they?'

Anne felt sorry for Wooldridge, his beloved papers summarily dismissed. 'This one isn't the one he was talking about at the house warming,' she pointed out.

'What a memory the girl's got,' Andy jibed.

'It's certainly a feat to be able to distinguish one of Wooldridge's papers from another,' Michael agreed.

'Especially after hours on end of Matron,' Meg added. 'I am so dreadfully sorry, Anne, that you were stuck with her all that time. I should have realised sooner. Really, she is a menace, the way she plants herself by the door and pounces.'

'It didn't matter,' Anne said easily. 'She was all right, really.' She spoke lazily. She

64

was content. Comfortable, relaxed, the cool evening light promised much, and yet nothing that she had to make any effort to attain. It was here within her grasp, everything that life could offer.

Michael's eyes seldom left her. In this mood of ease, in her loose silk shift, flowing, informal, he saw her as soft and desirable. All that he had felt and had suppressed in the past months rose in him again, stronger and more urgent through its period of denial. Unknown to him, his feelings for Anne had been leading a life of their own during the intervening time. They had matured and deepened. There was no doubt in his mind now.

When he offered to drive her home, Anne had no doubt either. She sat in his car, calm with confident anticipation.

He drove away from the Taussigs' towards the heath. Uphill past the sleeping Vale of Health – it was early morning – the car climbed towards Whitestone Pond. Michael turned east in the direction of Highgate, and pulled into the side of the road.

Without a word, they both stepped out. From the heath beneath them – they were almost at its highest point – the fresh country smell of night in the woods and the long grass came to meet them, and an owl called.

He gave her no time to wonder. His arms came round her. Then his hands, gentle still, came discovering her cheeks, her brow, the nape of her neck, then tilted her head to meet his, and they locked in an embrace the more profound for being so long deferred.

The understanding between them was to be all that Anne had dreamed. Now began those days that she had so often imagined in the past months, and so often cursed herself for imagining. Days through which she was companioned by Michael. Days when she turned to him for advice, looked for his tall spare figure as she walked down a corridor at the Central, and he was there. Saved a joke to tell him, and an hour later he was with her, enjoying it. Thought of a drive to the country, and he appeared, offering it.

Michael liked to leave London and the hospital behind, and to take her out into the cool downland for the day, driving competently, without fuss, in his sleek black Rover.

She was to find though, that he was essentially urban. He liked, for instance, a good lunch in a first-class hotel. Before she realised this, she packed new rolls, cheese, olives and a flask of strong black coffee, with half a dozen cans of beer, for them to have a meal in the open. But though he put a good face on it, he was obviously uneasy during the expedition, looking fastidiously for some way of wiping his sticky fingers, fidgeting on the uneven ground, inspecting his legs for insects. Anne never repeated the picnic. Nor did she repeat the casual clothes she had worn then, when she had gone comfortably attired in jeans, sandals, and a gingham shirt, carrying a sweater to pull on when it grew cooler. She soon saw that Michael liked to show her off in the hotels they visited. A freshly-ironed cotton dress might just make the grade, but a linen suit, with exactly the right blouse, was distinctly better. These, though, were minor adjustments. Through the long settled days of that lovely summer, she and Michael shared their lives and were happy together.

By contrast the Taussigs appeared to be quarrelling more bitterly. One night, driving home from the house in Hampstead, Michael and Anne discussed the situation. The quarrel, this time, had blown up as the result of something Anne had said. She had been talking about Onajianya and Clare, wanting, in fact, Michael's opinion on their growing friendship. Andy had interrupted, saying, 'This is simply colour prejudice, Anne. How hypocritical you English are.'

'No,' Anne had protested. She was sure Andy was wrong. 'It's nothing to do with colour. I should feel the same if Onajianya had been – say – Russian. Mixed marriages, marriages between people of different cultures, different languages, are frighteningly hard to manage.'

'It's nonsense to pretend–'

'This is reality,' Anne urged. 'It's a risk and a risk taken in ignorance.'

'So what?' Michael asked lazily. 'Life's full of risks. It's their affair. You can't provide safety for those you happen to know. Not your business to interfere.'

'But I see *exactly* why Anne feels she can't simply stand aside and do nothing, while someone too young to know what she's letting herself in for completely *ruins* her life,' Meg agreed.

'So that's what you think you did?' Andy demanded viciously. 'And you're wishing Anne had stepped in then and stopped you from being such a fool as to marry anyone as unsatisfactory as me, eh? Would have saved you a great deal of trouble, if Anne had stopped you ruining *your* life, when you were too young to know what *you* were doing. I suppose?' His hostile glance flicked angrily from Meg to Anne and back again to Meg.

Michael and Anne had escaped as soon as they could. They had both been embarrassed at the naked emotion Andy had displayed. Driving from Haverstock Hill towards central London and Anne's flat, Michael had let out a deep breath of relief. 'That was difficult,' he said. 'That marriage is shortly going to bust up completely. And a good thing, too. It's bad for both of them.'

'But people have been saying that for years.'

'It will now.'

'Why now, if it didn't before? Things are much better now – materially, I mean. Life's much easier for both of them.'

'That's probably why. They've time now to brew up resentment, perhaps. Until now, they've had to break away from each other to go to work, or for Andy to study for some exam. They've both always been absolutely determined to fulfil their outside commit-ments.' This was true. The marriage had been stormy from the beginning. One of them had often rushed out in a rage, banging doors. But when they met again so much would have happened to them that the earlier quarrel meant little. It had become trivial, hardly remembered. Not – usually – resolved, merely abandoned. And throughout everything, they both shared one aim, whatever occurred, to make a career for Andy.

'Andy's taken dreadful advantage of Meg, always,' Anne pointed out.

'She's the sort who wants to be taken advantage of,' Michael retorted, and shrugged. 'That's her look-out. Anyway, no advantage is at present being taken – hence the upsets. And hence, I am willing to prophesy, the end of the marriage.'

'Do you think that now Andy's got all he wanted out of her, he'll break it up deliberately? Is that what he was up to, tonight?'

Michael shrugged again. 'Who can tell?'

Anne sighed. 'I don't know whether to hope they end it or not. In some ways I should be relieved to see Meg right out of it, free to make a decent life for herself. But so much unhappiness would come first. I don't know.'

'There's nothing you can do.'

'I always feel perhaps there might be, and I'm failing to do it.'

'Can't live other people's lives for them. Probably make matters worse, not better, if you interfere. The safest thing is to keep out.

It's always a mistake to interfere in marriages. Let them work it out for themselves.'

'But–'

'Got our own lives to live. And very nice too.' He smiled at her, took her hand. 'I like that dress,' he remarked. 'It suits you. Ought to get some more like it.'

Anne had been surprised when he first commented on her dresses. She had not supposed Michael to be the sort of man to take much interest in clothes. But he showed himself to have decided views, criticising and advising on colour and line. He made her buy soft colours, grey, cinnamon, heather or beige, and dresses that flowed. It was a year of elegance in fashion, when cut was simple and long, colours muted. Dress, stockings, gloves, bag, all had to match or blend. Michael approved of this, especially for Anne.

Life with Michael revolutionised her appearance. Gone were the chic tailormades of clear colours, with crisp little touches of pale blue or tan, that Anne considered she looked best in. Michael disagreed. 'Your looks, you know, are startling enough,' he said, to her amazement. Her looks, startling? She scrutinised herself in the bathroom mirror. Nothing there to startle her. She had known it all for years, and it hadn't changed a bit. Good bones and a clear skin, that was all there was to be said. Nothing magical about her looks, she had always regretted. She was unaware of the light of her blue eyes and the gleam of her heavy hair. 'My golden girl,' Tim had called her. She remembered, of course, the term, but had forgotten that the expression held any meaning other than his love for her.

So now she was Michael's golden girl. It was a nourishing relationship, steady and affectionate. A comfortable, adult relationship, different entirely from the passionate madness, the ups and downs of life with Tim.

Under everyone's eyes she altered. Not only her clothes changed – though this alone was enough to set the entire staff at the Central speculating. She became noticeably more feminine, less controlled. She dashed about to shops or restaurants in her lunch hour, returning flushed, vibrant, with a new blouse, a dress, a pair of shoes, or an armful of flowers from Michael, alcohol on her breath and the smell of Michael's cigar on her clothes. She tore about matching silks to gloves, shoes, stockings, bags, and rushed off at odd moments to have her hair set.

For Michael had made her cut her hair. For years she had wound the golden pile round her head. This had begun when she first knew Tim. He had loved to play with her hair, to run it through his fingers. He had forbidden her to cut it, and she had become accustomed then to pushing it up and out of the way as she did her housework or went to the shops. As time went on she had learnt how to put it into a pleat. While Tim was alive the golden cap was always slipping, always out of control, escaping from its pins, or heavy and loose, flopping sideways over her high forehead. Since his death, she had learnt how to control her hair, the pleat had gained in security, and her coiffure became balanced, lacquered, immovable, untouched except by herself. Untouchable, some felt. Never, of course, unnoticeable. Hair of that colour, carried on a head like Anne's, cannot be that. Many men had toyed with the idea of pulling it out about her ears. Somehow the plans had come to nothing.

Now Michael made her cut it, made her wear it straight and loose, flopping about her eyes again. Once more she was unable to control it – and, as she complained, she had to spend pounds at the hairdresser. Those to whom she complained reassured her. The new style was a success, they all asserted. 'You look so much *younger*,' they cried with one voice.

'Humph,' Anne said. Had she previously looked the same age as Miss Glossop – or perhaps Lady Ramsay would be nearer the mark?

'You look so much less *severe*,' one candid friend added.

Anne wondered why friendship should extend to telling her this now, rather than mentioning it during the years that were past, advocating change, or alternatively remaining silent still? She asked herself, with some dismay, if that was how they had all thought of her – severe, even disapproving?

Unknown to herself, who felt so lacking in assurance, so imperfect, so unequal to the others, Anne provoked this reaction from many who knew her. She looked successful, well-groomed. She moved so effortlessly, they considered, through her world of colleagues, friendships, social occasions. She had her own flat, her own job, she knew everyone, she had travelled, she had money. She had been married to a promising young man. If she had not married again, it could only be by her own choice. Women were envious of her fragile elegance, and of her material security and independence.

Despite her beauty, though, men found her a good sort rather than a seductive girl friend. Unmistakably clever, she was a trifle exhausting. They liked to take her to the theatre or a dance when they wanted to create an impression, to show her off, but for making love most of them preferred a less rigid, more cosy, girl. They had none of them, apart from Meg, any inkling that to be Anne Heseltine did not feel in the least as they imagined.

Chapter 3

Jennifer Ramsay had worshipped Michael Vanstone for years. He had first come into her life when she was a pleasant child of eight, and he was her father's house physician. He had played with her, and talked to her as she grew older. He had shown her the gentle teasing affection that popular and sought-after young men often feel free to display towards attractive and privileged children. Now she had grown up, become a chic young girl, she still worshipped him. Sharing his own world of hospital as she did, her admiration for him doubled. And she trusted him utterly, as she had always done.

Michael Vanstone was admired by the girls who were training with Jennifer. It would be an immense triumph to become his girl friend – was already a triumph in the nurses' home to be escorted by him at all.

Jennifer was a plodder, she tried hard, and she was steadfast. Unknown to her contemporaries, she had a sneaking, hardly admitted feeling that she was not dominated as she assumed them to be by love or passion. She knew this was something to be ashamed of, that she was different, out of step – perhaps less mature? The knowledge made her more conventional, imitative. She conformed as far as possible to what she didn't quite succeed in understanding. Not being led by her heart, she was yet determined to find love or admiration – for her, at present, the two were indistinguishable.

But she found she could have about Michael Vanstone all those romantic feelings which in other cases she had merely imitated. He was her hero, her pulse quickened when he was in the ward. When he met her in the evening, she knew herself to be genuinely excited. Her life then was as she wished it to be.

She decided she must be in love with Michael.

Was he going to take her seriously? Or did he still think of her as a child? Could she hold him against other and far more sophisticated girls? Against women of his own age? (Anne Heseltine, she meant, though she pretended to herself that he had no one especially in mind.) Finding her grown-up, a schoolgirl no longer, was it possible that he would at last ask her to marry him? She waited, sometimes hopefully, sometimes in agony, for this to occur.

After the Taussigs' housewarming party, she had been elated. Not only had Michael come at once to talk to her when she had arrived, he had driven her down to the Central – where, delivered at the nurses' home by Michael Vanstone in his Rover, she had been the envy of them all. Then, after midnight, he had appeared in the ward and had spent an hour talking to her. In fact, it was plain to anyone that he could not keep away from her. Flushed and hopeful, she shone with success.

For Michael, though, Jennifer was still discernibly the charming schoolgirl, earnest and touching, trying very hard to be grown-up, trying very hard altogether – not now at her lessons, but at her duties as a nurse. He enjoyed looking after her, helping her. He liked taking her about. She was a sweet child, well turned out and charming, who deferred to him, made no demands. When he went into the wards, and saw her trim young figure bustling about, with a slight but unmistakable air of self-importance, he felt at home, and comfortably aware of his own distinction.

His feelings for Anne Heseltine were different. With Anne he was in love, almost unwillingly in love, an emotion strong enough to be strange to him. On the evening of the Taussigs' first party in their new house, he had been swept off his feet by her beauty, and his relationship with her had suddenly seemed of vital importance.

His only reason for looking for Jennifer that night had been to talk to her, to use her as an audience. He wanted to talk himself out of his obsession with Anne. That this might be unfair to Jennifer did not cross his mind, and after spending some time with her, he had gone to have a further look at his patient. Then he had returned home to bed, no longer obsessed, but very certain of his love for Anne.

The next morning he had gone early to the Central to see how the child was doing. Afterwards he had driven to the country to see a private patient. He had returned late in the evening, tired, completely wrapped up in questions of clinical medicine. He had made some notes, looked up a few points, telephoned one or two colleagues, and he had been about to go to bed when Wooldridge had telephoned to say he thought their patient was dying. He had gone over to the

Central at once, and he and Derek, after a battle, had, as he had known they inevitably must, lost the little girl. Michael had spoken to her parents, a duty he dreaded, and did not do at all well, but which his sense of obligation would not allow him to delegate to Derek – who, as it happened, was quite good at it.

By this time it was early morning, and too late to go to bed. He had returned to his flat, had a bath and a large breakfast. Then he went back to the Central for a ward round, attended not only by the usual students, but by two American colleagues whom he had afterwards lunched. In the afternoon he had seen private patients at his consulting-rooms in Wimpole Street, and had dictated letters to his secretary there. Afterwards he went round the corner to the Royal Society of Medicine for a drink and a meal, intending to look into the library to check a few references, and then return home for an early night. However, he met too many people he knew, and found himself involved in a long argument about controlled trials of a drug he was interested in. It was after midnight when he left. At last, then, he had gone home to bed.

When he woke the following day he was,

not altogether surprisingly, drained of all energy, all emotion. His earlier love for Anne appeared to him now imaginary, mistaken, demanding more than he could give.

For this reason he had kept away from her. He meant all his actions for the best. He assumed that his feelings on the night of the party had been apparent to no one, and that they had better remain in that state. He dared not trust himself with Anne, for fear his body led him into an unwanted situation, and he turned to what he thought to be the safety of Jennifer. He never guessed that here he was implying a readiness to become all too permanently involved.

Hospital gossip, because of his past affairs with women, coupled with his successful evasion of matrimony, credited him with far more calculation than he had, and far more sophistication. Professional success had come to him early, though not perhaps as effortlessly as they all imagined. Now they considered him capable of an equally effortless management of any women in his life. They thought, too, that he must be well aware that Jennifer Ramsay was his for the taking.

This he did not know. Jennifer, he supposed, had boy friends of her own age. Soon she would have no time for him, so much her senior. In happy ignorance he continued to escort her and to drop in on her in the wards, while the hospital watched. 'My dear,' they said, 'of course he's serious *this* time. He'd never dream of anything else with Ramsay's daughter. Ramsay was his chief – made him. Now he's going to marry the chief's daughter, like any up-and-coming young man with his ears pinned back. And why not? I think she's sweet – and she adores him, so what could be better?'

Meanwhile Lady Ramsay took Jennifer off to Switzerland on holiday, joining a party of friends there. Jennifer was preoccupied still with Michael. She observed the love affairs of the group of young people in the party dispassionately. Uninterested in any of the men, she soon acquired the reputation of being a good sport (though hopelessly cold and inhibited, they all agreed), who could be relied on not to be jealous, who would willingly make herself scarce when necessary, or alternatively make a third when this was required. The girls confided in her (not that she understood a word, they often felt) and so did the men.

As a result, Jennifer began to do some hard thinking. Innocent and sheltered, the only child of elderly and conventional parents, until now it had never occurred to her that she could 'do anything' about men. Either they were attracted or they weren't.

Now she saw that this was not necessarily the case. Other girls forced events – and men – into their own desired pattern. Other girls chased after men who attracted them, and though people laughed about it, often made unkind jokes, the fact remained that the girl often seemed to get the man she chased. What was more, contrary to common mythology, it was quite obvious that men enjoyed being chased.

Jennifer returned home from Switzerland determined to begin chasing Michael Vanstone. She wished she had thought of this possibility long ago.

One week-end soon after her return he went down to Densworth, the Ramsays' country house outside Haslemere. There was nothing unusual about this. He had been in the habit of spending occasional week-ends there since he had been Uncle Alec's houseman. What was more unusual was that Jennifer had gone to enormous lengths of duplicity and perseverance, had in fact made herself thoroughly unpopular, in order to have the same week-end free.

Michael was nice to her, as always. He joked with her, played tennis, took her for walks. 'You young people,' Lady Ramsay said, pairing them off. She had never fully grasped that Michael was no longer Uncle Alec's raw young houseman, though she considered he had become very presentable these days.

Jennifer weighed and considered every sentence they exchanged, every glance Michael gave her, every light word he uttered – praise for a good stroke at tennis, a quick repartee, admiration for a charming dress in the evening. Yes, she decided, he must be interested in her. But he was a confirmed bachelor. Everyone said so. She must be the one to make the advances, or else they could go on in this friendly way for ever. It would do Michael good to marry and settle down.

By the time he drove her back to London on Sunday night the whole affair was settled in her own mind. She treated him in a possessive manner, which Lady Ramsay noticed at once. She made her mother book Michael for another week-end before he left, and stood over them watching them write it in their diaries.

Then she took to telephoning Michael from the nurses' home and asking him to take her out. Michael was amused and flattered. He was also very fully booked. Once or twice, partly because he was touched by Jennifer's approach, and partly because he thought he owed it to Uncle Alec to look after Jennifer when required, he cancelled an evening with Anne.

'He's running them both,' they said at the Central. 'How long does he think he can get away with that?'

The next week-end at Densworth came. Jennifer was determined to clinch matters. After a dinner in which she knew she had looked her best, and an evening spent playing scrabble, she said good night earlier than usual and went to have her bath. She powdered herself all over with her mother's talc, scented herself with her mother's toilet water, put on a new nightdress she had bought for the occasion, set her hair and lacquered it, and – hardly tripped, advanced purposefully with a firm tread, like a nurse down a ward, along the corridor to Michael's room, opened the door and went in.

Michael, not unnaturally, was taken by surprise, and was too startled to take evasive action. He was also charmed by her, though at the same time terrified. With reason, as he was to discover.

'Michael, darling,' Jennifer breathed in best starlet manner, 'you are so *dreadfully* attractive. I simply *had* to come and see you – we never have a chance to be *alone*. You don't mind, do you?' She snuggled trustfully up to him, wafting fumes of Lady Ramsay's toilet water and Colgate toothpaste. Automatically, Michael put his arm round her – it seemed unfriendly not to, though afterwards he wondered if he had been hypnotised. At once she pressed her face firmly against his, and did her not unsuccessful best to melt into his arms. They did not remain unresponsive for long.

The next morning he wondered why he hadn't pushed her straight out of the room as soon as the door had opened. But the fact remained that he had not done so. What he had done, he told himself miserably, was to seduce her under her own father's roof. He was conventionally convinced that because the episode occurred under this particular roof he was the more to blame. He was also, as he realised hollowly, more likely to be landed with the consequences.

At breakfast he was subdued, and could meet no one's eye. Even Lady Ramsay saw this, and assumed correctly that his behaviour was connected with her daughter. She conjectured that perhaps Jennifer had been running after poor Michael a little too blatantly, and the poor young man was becoming embarrassed. The exact form Jennifer's pursuit had taken was never to occur to her. She would have had a considerable shock. She complained to her husband merely that Jennifer had left the bathroom in uproar, and had helped herself to all her toilet water – had the wretched child bathed in it?

'And I'm afraid she's been teasing poor Michael. He was distinctly distrait and embarrassed this morning. Do you think she'd been a little too blatant? She does dote on him so.'

'She's growing up,' Uncle Alex said comfortably. 'No need to worry, though. Michael will look after her all right. Dependable.'

Jennifer was extremely smug and pleased with herself. She couldn't understand why Michael should be so peculiar this morning, but then men were well known to be odd. She went back on duty glowing with achievement. At last she was a woman. She had lost that juvenile possession, her out-dated virginity. She would understand now what they were all talking about. She would be able to join in the jokes. Did it all seem rather a fuss about nothing, not even very enjoyable at the time? It was true, though, that she felt marvellous today. But then of course she was changed. And she knew, too, that Michael loved her. He would, surely, in due course, marry her? There could be no doubt about that now. Here she was much luckier, she told herself, than other girls. They were often, according to what they confided, late at night, sprawling across one of the narrow beds in the nurses' home, very unfortunate in the man who was their first lover. The first time was important, was meant to be something special, they all agreed. For her it was. For some girls it was a casual affair only, and this was not at all the same thing. Because they all concurred about this. You could never forget the first one. (Most of them, of course, had had no more than a matter of months in which to achieve forgetfulness.)

For her it was Michael. For her it would always be Michael. She knew, too, that he would never let her down. Soon he would marry her. After all, it would be insane of him to have become involved with her in her own home unless he intended to marry her. And no one had ever suggested that Michael was insane. Quite the contrary. After all, he could not afford to let her down, a realistic voice reprimanded her.

Perhaps she might even be going to have a baby, she thought hopefully. That would make matters certain beyond doubt, and would also have the pleasing effect of hurrying events forward. Yes, on the whole it would be an excellent idea to have a baby.

Here she underestimated Michael's caution. He might have lost his head the previous evening, but he was not completely lost to all sense of reality. What had happened was bad enough, he thought wryly, as he drove frowning back to London. Here was he, Michael Vanstone, said to be sophisticated, worldly, well-established in his career, with the Chair of Medicine ready to drop into his waiting hands – and he had to fall into the oldest trap of all. He was involved with chief's daughter, and he couldn't see how the hell he was to get out of it without losing the Chair at the same time. Why in God's name hadn't he simply turned the tiresome baggage right about as soon as she had opened his door, smacked her on the bottom as she deserved, and sent her on her way?

Unfortunately he hadn't. So now here he was, not only mistakenly, inadvertently, involved with Jennifer Ramsay, but also in the well-known and foolish position of being tied to two women. Moreover, two women – well, all right, what if one was a child? That made it worse – who knew one another, moved in the same world, worked in the same hospital. How had he ever allowed this to happen.

Somehow he must extricate himself.

Somehow, though, he didn't. His life turned into a morass of deceit, of cancelled appointments. He was always going off to collect Jennifer from the nurses' home, having rehearsed what he wanted to say. He would explain that there was nothing in it, they must stop seeing each other. It wasn't fair to her to go on like this. She must look for someone her own age, and forget about him. He had been selfish and thoughtless, and it would never happen again.

The trouble was that it did happen again. He seemed unable to deliver his rehearsed speech to Jennifer, and then, after the theatre, the meal, the opera, or whatever it was they had done in the evening she would demand confidently, her eyes shining, limpid with love, that they went back to his flat, because she had a late pass and it was still terribly early. He never meant to take her there, and sometimes he succeeded in refusing, in pleading work to do, a case to see in the wards, or a patient to visit in the London Clinic. But he didn't evade her often enough. To his despair he found himself, six weeks after the week-end at Densworth, still carrying on with two women.

Not only was he tormented by his failure to extricate himself from his association with Jennifer, but he was in a state of confusion and self-disgust. He had been shown an aspect of his character that he had never suspected. What sort of a man was he? Was he a weakling, who lacked the determination to rid himself of a naïve young girl, and instead harmed her, deceived her, led her on? Or was he a gay philanderer? He could hardly have felt less gay. Was he, simply, a worthless drifter? Or a conscienceless opportunist? And, for God's sake, what about his career. Thinking of his career, what about Ramsay? What about his duty to the old man, who had trained him, and whose protégé he had been from the beginning? Was this the way to treat Ramsay's only daughter, seducing her weekly in his own flat? She was an ignorant girl barely out of her teens. He ought to be treating her like an elder brother. Like an uncle. He ought to talk to her like a Dutch uncle. The phrase suddenly popped into his mind.

Why a Dutch uncle, he wondered? How had that nomenclature become accepted? His questioning, analytical brain safely side-tracked him from the point at issue and lowered the emotional temperature for him. He went in search of a dictionary.

Michael constantly dissipated emotion in analysis, genuine outbursts of feeling in prolonged intellectual questioning. But whatever the result of his self-communion, he could not be said to be enjoying his sex-life. It was too much for him.

At least there was safety with Anne. She was his own age, his loving, understanding comforter. As long as she didn't understand too much – the affair with Jennifer, for instance. She would, he knew, be deeply hurt if she found out about this situation. But then at present he was taking care that she knew nothing about it. Apart from his worry here, he had no feeling of responsibility for her, of the kind he had for Jennifer. He was not, he felt, deceiving her. His love for her was straightforward, and reciprocated hers for him. No cause for shame here.

Only with Jennifer was he in a false position. For after all, he cared little for her. She was a pretty young thing, and he would under other circumstances have been entirely happy to take her out now and again, even to avail himself of the attractive young body that was so blindly offered him. If only the girl had not been Ramsay's daughter. He knew himself a traitor to the old man, and yet he could not escape from Jennifer.

He began to dread her bright young gaze, perpetually meeting his with love and adoration. He feared her neat young figure as it bustled round the ward. Jennifer was far too correct to catch his eye on duty, but he always feared that one day she would do so. He dreaded the way her face lighted up when he met her, and he was tormented by the trust he saw there.

He went about harassed, pursued by his own conscience. Pursued, too, by the interested glances of his colleagues and the nursing staff. How long, they all wondered, would he be able to keep it up? Jennifer on Monday and Thursday, they enumerated spitefully, Anne on Tuesday and Friday, alternate week-ends – was Wednesday his night off, they asked one another, grinning? There was little hope of keeping your private life to yourself within signalling distance of the Central. The spy system there could have taught the Kremlin a thing or two about constant surveillance. Did he perhaps keep another girl friend hidden away for Wednesday nights? A rumour grew that the third girl did indeed exist, left over from the days before he had become involved with either Jennifer or Anne, tucked away somewhere out of sight – like an Edwardian mistress in St John's Wood, perhaps? She must, they agreed, be getting a little annoyed at being cut down to Wednesdays only. One must assume, too, that Vanstone would hardly be a particularly vigorous performer on this weekly visit, in view of his other commitments. The regular girl friend, in fact, might shortly be expected to begin making scenes. She might appear in the Central to make them. 'And that won't be very good for his chances of the Chair, will it? What will Uncle Alex say, for one thing?'

Another group discounted the existence of the regular girl friend. 'Let the poor chap have a night off, to catch up on the *Lancet* and write up his notes,' they said. 'Michael Vanstone's no fool. He got rid of the old girl friend before starting on the new.' The theory here was that Anne Heseltine had replaced the girl friend, and was, as one might say, for fun. Jennifer, as they had always assumed, was for settling down, marriage, and a career.

To his own dismay, this was how the situation was beginning to strike Michael himself. He turned away in disgust each time the notion struck him. Yet it had to be admitted, this would be a solution. This was a method of keeping everyone happy, and getting the Chair into the bargain.

It was a nasty shock to him when not only did Anne's father, hitherto safely out of reach in Australia, appear on the scene at emphatically an awkward moment, but that he turned out to be almost as powerful and influential a figure as Ramsay himself. This was a jolting and unforeseen complication.

The realisation hit him during one of the committee meetings of the Nyganda Foundation. How he had failed to understand before this who Anne's father was he could not later imagine. When Anne had mentioned her father in conversation, Michael had naturally asked her what he did these days. He had known, of course, that he had once been at the Central. Anne had said, 'Oh, he's a surgeon, in Sydney, you know.' As she made this remark, she had given him an odd look, which he had failed to interpret. As it happened she had been giving her inherited Australian humour an unexpected airing. Murray Colegate was a urological surgeon of international standing. He had been responsible for the first successful kidney graft in the southern hemisphere, at a time when the number of these grafts anywhere in the world could be counted on the fingers of one hand. The press had made much of the operation – of the surgeon, of the hospital, of the patient, who had been a young Australian of wealthy background. Murray Colegate was far from being a nonentity. But Michael had never known Anne's surname before her marriage to Tim Heseltine, and he had shown no particular interest in her family. Somehow he had never visualised her Australian father as part of their world. How wrong he had been he was now to find out. He sat brooding, ashamed, at the committee table. The smooth young consultant, he was thinking, Michael Vanstone, D.M., F.R.C.P., forging his way steadily to the top, almost certainly the next Professor of Medicine – oh yeah? Instead there was a quivering oaf, cringing between two enormous figures, two distinguished men towering over him, a shotgun wedding – two shotgun weddings. He had to marry Jennifer Ramsay and Anne Heseltine at one and the same moment.

The Nyganda Foundation Executive Committee was a friendly, informal little group. It met monthly, and there were only, including the chairman and secretary, eight members. Of these, only two were women, Miss Glossop and Mrs Heseltine. This left Anne as the only representative with any claim to feminine charm, and the committee was in the habit, while it paused for coffee, of playing up to her a little – especially as the chairman was known to be fond of her, to have, as they said, 'a soft spot for Anne Heseltine'. They made a slight fuss of her often, and encouraged her to lighten the official tone of the proceedings. On this occasion, in the course of the discussion about the nurse-training school to be opened in Nyganda, for which Miss Glossop had been lobbying so busily and which had been duly placed early in the agenda, there had been general complaint about the behaviour of newly-arrived students. Members of the committee took the opportunity to air, over the coffee cups, some of their perennial grumbles about difficult students, especially those from overseas.

'Too big for their boots.'

'They seem to think it's extremely good of them to come to our horrible inhospitable country.'

'Then the next thing is they *will not* go home.'

'Arrogant.'

'Always showing off.'

'Infernally pleased with themselves.'

Ann began to defend them. 'You know,' she pointed out – how many times had she said it? 'I don't honestly think they mean to be arrogant. It's simply that it *is* an achievement to get there. They've tried awfully hard to arrive, and suddenly, here they are. They're overwhelmed with the importance of it. They've been especially chosen to come here, and they're determined to make good, and to show everybody how right the choice has been. In a way, there'd be something wrong with them if they didn't show off a bit.'

'Something in that,' Marlow, the heart surgeon, agreed. 'It usually does wear off. I think it's rather the equivalent of first-night nerves. The ones who display them often do best, once they've settled.'

'Of course, it's not by any means confined to Nygandans,' Ramsay said. 'It's common, surely, to most newly-arrived students? Students *are* arrogant. They've all been big fishes in little ponds.'

'Students from Nyganda are apt to take

longer to notice that they're in a big pond now,' Michael remarked.

'It's true that overseas visitors in general often give us this impression of arrogance, not to mention disgruntlement,' Marlow said. 'I'm afraid I do find it irritating, though usually it's the result of a determination to conceal their own insecurity,' he added with a broad grin. 'I try to remember this – I find it helps me.' He laughed.

'My father,' Ann said, 'always swears that when he first arrived from Australia, he was tremendously opinionated. Looking back, he says, its sticks out a mile. He says he was conceited and incredibly outspoken. But at the time he was quite unaware of this, he's convinced. Of course,' she said with a reminiscent smile, 'Australians, as everyone knows, are a rude lot, and it's come to be expected of them. I think they play up to it. It's their trademark – a national characteristic, like English reserve. Now, in the Nygandans–'

Ramsay interrupted her. 'You know, you do your father an injustice,' he said, taking the sting from the words with a benevolent gleam from under his heavy brows. 'He made a far better impression than his daughter seems to think.' He looked round the table, collecting eyes, deciding that this was a useful opportunity both to boost Anne's standing with the committee before his own retirement, and to remind them of Murray Colegate's long connection with the Central, where he had trained. 'He was, of course, immediately recognised as the outstanding student of his year, so he had something to be conceited about. Except that as a matter of fact he wasn't particularly conceited. Probably because, like many really able young men, he knew how much he had to learn. Outspoken, yes. And what he was inclined to do – I agree with you there – was to brandish his uncomfortable brand of humour at inconvenient times – still does, bless him.' He ruminated. No one interrupted. 'Of course,' he said, waking up, 'Mrs Heseltine's father, as perhaps not everyone realises, is Murray Colegate.' He then led the talk back to the agenda and the training school, oblivious of the effect of what had undoubtedly been a small bombshell.

Miss Glossop swivelled her protuberant grey eyes immediately to Michael Vanstone. 'Let's see how you take that, young man.' She was pleased to note that he looked, first, startled out of his wits, and then distinctly alarmed. And so you should be, she thought to herself. That'll teach you to play fast and loose. For Miss Glossop had been – not shocked, matrons of large general hospital are normally immune to shock – disappointed, perhaps. She had had faith in Michael Vanstone. Had she not repeatedly said so? Perhaps success had come too easily, too young. But he had seemed so ready for it. Ready, too, for the Chair of Medicine.

Miss Glossop had, as she had remarked generally round the hospital, approved of what she regarded as his courtship of Jennifer Ramsay. When the affair with Anne Heseltine had begun, she had been amazed, and was at first inclined to blame Anne. But she had been forced to remain on good terms with the girl. The Nyganda training school was after all more important than any of the love affairs of silly young doctors and guileless female members of the staff. She had slowly come to feel sympathy for her. Anne Heseltine was blooming. She looked quite different. Anyone could see that. But then so was poor young Jennifer Ramsay. Both of them, Miss Glossop confided to her friend the matron of St Peter's, in happy ignorance of the other. 'That wretched man,' she had exclaimed, 'of course, he's going to marry Jennifer Ramsay, any fool can see that. It's poor Mrs Heseltine, already a widow, who's going to be left alone again. *And* made to look a fool into the bargain. Because don't tell me that keen young man is going to ditch Professor Ramsay's daughter, just now, of all times. Oh dear me, no. He knows which side his bread is buttered, none better.'

For Miss Glossop too had known nothing about Anne's father. So he was Murray Colegate, was he? Just like the girl never to have said so. Imagine her being his daughter. Cheeky young man. She remembered him as a houseman. Of course, there was a family likeness, now she came to think of it. She was irritated with herself for having known nothing of the relationship. She must be losing her grip. Anyway, Michael Vanstone wouldn't find it quite so easy to have a quiet affair on the side with Murray Colegate's daughter, and then be off to make the grade with Professor Ramsay and Jennifer. How are you going to get out of that one, she wondered? Especially as Murray Colegate knew the Ramsay's well. Now we *shall* see, Miss Glossop thought.

Michael Vanstone thought so too. She had gauged his feelings correctly. He had hardly realised, until Ramsay's words showed him that his intentions would be difficult to carry out, what they had been. But his immediate reaction to the news was, 'Oh God, how am I going to get out of it now?'

He sickened himself. Had he indeed been planning to drop Anne? And this merely because he thought he could get away with it, in order to marry the Professor's daughter and more or less inherit the Chair of Medicine? Surely, he thought, shocked, this is none of I? But self-examination told him this was exactly what he had been planning. True, he had not himself been responsible for Jennifer's pursuit of him. This had been unsought, unwelcome, inescapable.

But why inescapable, he asked himself bitterly? Simply because he knew it was to his advantage not to break with the child. Have you no humanity, no genuine feelings? He had always imagined himself to be scrupulous.

He remained in the worst of tempers for several days, and saw neither Anne nor Jennifer. The hospital was vastly amused. The story of Anne's distinguished parentage had gone round like wildfire.

Anne herself, as luck would have it, was too busy to be bothered by Michael's temporary absence. Colegate and her stepmother had arrived, had been met by her at the airport and seen into their room at the

English-Speaking Union in Charles Street, where they always stayed. Presents were given, meals eaten, family news exchanged. Now the real entertaining was beginning, with lunches, dinners, lectures and surgery for Murray Colegate, and shopping expeditions and sightseeing for Anne and Lady Colegate. All this, of course, in addition to work. Anne was hoping to take a holiday later, to go to Cornwall with the Colegates – Murray had booked all the rooms at his favourite little hotel there for a month, and intended to return hospitality in this way.

Clare, usually a tower of strength, chose this moment to announce her engagement to Dr Onajianya, and to become, it appeared, completely distracted. Anne was divided between sympathy and irritation. Clare's parents in Devonshire were horrified at the prospect of having an African son-in-law and grandchildren, and Clare was continually being demoralised by letters and telephone calls from them, begging her to reconsider her decision, after which she invariably dropped whatever she had been doing and rushed to Onajinaya for support. They were both intending to go to Nyganda shortly, and Clare was buying suitable clothes and writing letters to her future relations there. The hospital thought the marriage a mistake, and said so, in no uncertain terms, to both Onajianya and Clare, so that they became edgy and aggressive. Clare's work became not only intermittent but totally unreliable, and Anne had not the heart to scold her, either about this or about her intended marriage. She should, she realised sadly, have had a straight talk with her before matters had gone so far. She felt that she had failed Clare.

Bill Barham returned from Nyganda at last, ebullient as ever, roaring with happy laughter over the bribery, which he had himself discovered before leaving. Anne wanted to warn him that it might not be as amusing as he thought, but when he took her out to dinner to celebrate his return (on an evening when the Colegates were attending a formal dinner at one of the colleges, to which Anne had not been invited) she could not bear the mar the occasion. She could not be the harbinger of defeat. She could not bring herself to warn him that they were all saying that he now had no hope of the Chair. Instead, she unburdened herself of her worries about Clare.

'Something must be done,' Bill said at once. 'Can't let them do that. Neither of the poor saps has an inkling of what they're letting themselves in for.'

'But, Bill,' Anne said in a worried voice, 'have we any right to interfere?'

He put his head back and laughed. 'You've been seeing too much of Michael Vanstone,' he announced. 'That's what's wrong with you. That's the brilliant pedant all over. "Don't do anything, in case it turns out to be the wrong thing. Keep your fingers clean at all costs. I'm all right, Jack".' Bill had no knowledge of Anne's intimacy with Michael. His intention was simply to ridicule her attitude by comparing it with Michael's, which he had always despised.

Anne, however, gaped. How had he found out? She had told him nothing about herself and Michael, though she had been afraid he might not approve of her choice. Certainly she had always intended to tell him. Bill was one of her oldest friends. But she had not so far had the opportunity – could people possibly have been talking, she wondered?

'Well, listen to me, my girl, for a change,' Bill was saying. 'Have we any right *not* to interfere? Tell me that.'

'Well,' Anne began dubiously, only to be interrupted.

'For God's sake, Anne. Been married yourself, after all. Wasn't all beer and skittles, was it? Damn difficult job. Can be worthwhile. Don't think I don't know that. But you need to be, first of all, exceptionally lucky. Then you have to have iron determination, and one of you at least should be an outstandingly nice person, unselfish, long-suffering, tolerant. H'm?'

Anne began laughing. 'It's not as bad as that,' she protested.

'Let's face it,' he retorted, 'most marriages, after the first ten years, have degenerated to the stage where the couple is reduced to making the best of a bad job.' He paused. 'You and I were unlucky in one way,' he said. 'But I occasionally wonder if we were luckier than we knew? We both lost our partners before we found out what the years would do to us. We missed them like hell, when they were snatched away, yet, you know...' he frowned, and drew a pattern on the tablecloth with his fork, his square, determined face suddenly sad and vulnerable, his eyes soft with memories. 'I sometimes wonder, I ask myself, what stage Phil and I would have reached by now, if she had lived?' He pondered. Phillipa Barham, a Queen Alexandra nursing sister, had been killed at Anzio, where she had been attending the wounded.

'Our marriage lasted only three years, and wartime years at that. Just brief leaves, you know, days off, sleeping out passes in dreary hotels. It was wonderful, though.' He flushed suddenly. 'Remembering makes me feel old. I've never felt like that since.' He sighed. 'I ought to have married again, within a year or two. Raised a family. I'd have liked children. But at the time I couldn't bring myself to do it. A mistake, really.'

Anne looked past him into her own dreams. She wanted to help Bill, in his sudden exposure of a loneliness she had never, in her selfishness, she thought painfully, suspected. Dear Bill, so full of vitality that no one felt sorry for him, missing Phillipa all these years. But his own sadness infected her, and she could not trust herself to speak for thinking of her own loss. Darling Tim. No one could ever take his place.

Bill cut into her thoughts. 'Never mind all that,' he remarked briskly. 'Point is, marriage is difficult. Young people always jumping in the deep end, haven't learnt to swim. Their elders and betters can see they're hopelessly unsuited. Often nothing we can do about it, of course. They just have to find out the hard way. But when two young people from totally different societies propose to embark on marriage, and far from being in the least deterred by the increased difficulty they face, we know it's the complication itself that's blinding them by its apparent glamour – *then*, I say, there's no doubt at all. It's time to step in and make them pause somewhat for reflection.'

'Pause?'

'Yes, pause. I'm not suggesting that we should try to prevent them marrying, only saying we should give them an opportunity for a little quiet reflection – preferably as far apart from each other as possible.'

'That's an idea.'

'Can we send Clare home to her people?'

'I don't know if she'd go,' Anne said doubtfully. 'I don't think I would, in her place. And if I did, I'd go absolutely determined to be unaffected by – oh, you know, old-fashioned parental prejudices.'

Bill laughed. 'Something in what you say,' he agreed. 'Though I can't quite fit that label on to Murray Colegate. How is the old devil?'

'Oh, in fine form.'

'Looking forward to meting him again – it's to be tomorrow evening, I gather, at Uncle Alec's.'

'Oh, are you going to be there, Bill? I am

glad. That'll be nice.'

'Looking forward to it immensely,' he said.

Michael Vanstone was not. He was dreading the encounter. When it came, it fulfilled his worst forebodings. He found himself at the dinner-table with two prospective fathers-in-law glaring across at him, one his host, the other the guest of honour. Worst of all, though, Lady Ramsay had seated him between Jennifer and Anne.

Andy Taussig, also at the dinner, was cynically amused to discover the situation, and kept sending an unresponsive Meg wild signals of ill-controlled merriment. Andy, of course, revelled in this sort of embarrassment. Meg, though, was filled with anxiety and dismay on Anne's behalf. She was sure Anne had no idea that Michael was still going around with Jennifer, and she experienced pangs of deep affection and protectiveness towards her, as she saw her, sitting there on one side of Michael, who was sharing his conversation – with a slightly farouche air, and could you wonder? – between the two girls. Lady Ramsay had spotlighted a situation everyone was longing to discuss. The story would be round the hospital tomorrow – one of Lady Ramsay's more monumental gaffes.

Meg was sitting next to Bill Barham herself, and in a quiet moment mentioned this to him – they all knew how good with people Bill was, and how knowledgeably kind. He had always been fond of Anne. Perhaps he would rescue her.

'One of Lady R's monumental gaffes,' she said in a low voice to him, glancing across the table at the ill-assorted trio.

'H'm? Has she done it again? Tell me all about it at once. I must catch up on all the gossip, I'm out of touch.' His green eyes sparkled. Bill enjoyed the interplay of personalities at the Central.

'It's Michael, stuck paralytically between Anne and Jennifer.'

'What's that?' he asked sharply, his eyes frosting. 'Why paralytically? What's that cold fish been up to now?'

Meg told him. To her amazement Bill was rigid with fury. Bill was always apt to react twice as vehemently as anyone else, and his rages were renowned. Meg saw uneasily that he was in the midst of one now. If she hadn't seen it, she would have felt it. Great gusts of it came from his sturdy, dinner-jacketed figure. She hoped he wasn't going to lean across the table and throttle Michael.

'I shouldn't have told you,' she said

111

belatedly, in a small voice.

'Oh yes, you should,' he said gratingly. 'Making her look a fool all over the hospital,' he added. 'Not to mention–' he broke off, scowling, to think it all out. Apparently, while he had been in Nyganda, Anne had become involved with that pedant Vanstone. She couldn't have picked anyone less suitable. What fools women could be. A good sign, in one sense, though. She was evidently recovering from Tim's death, was ready for a new union. That was as it should be. Healthy. But she must be detached from Vanstone as soon as possible, and with as little trauma as possible. Because he would be no use to her – had already, it seemed, done her harm. Made her the centre of a funny story to be related round the hospital.

At this point his searing rage astonished Bill himself almost as much as it did Meg. It hurt him to know that Anne was being treated in this way, and he urgently desired to punish Vanstone. After her years of loneliness, this was no way to begin again. Vanstone was a destroyer, an icy-fingered killer of the life of the heart. If he continued in this way, Anne would sooner or later find out her deception and retreat back into her loneliness, so wounded that she might not venture out again. If she discovered – or when she discovered, for she was bound to find out some time – that Vanstone had been playing with her feelings, would she be able, mistrustful as she already was, to believe in any man? After Tim, this.

Vanstone no doubt had his eye on the Chair of Medicine. This would be why he was stringing Jennifer Ramsay along. Typical. Bill's thoughts broke off in confusion, as consuming rage swept him again. With the rage came an iron determination to look after Anne, whether she wanted it or not. Somehow he was going to prevent her from being hurt. That was all there was to it. Right through him swept this wave of tenderness and anger, and though the anger was to ebb and flow, the tenderness stayed. It was this characteristic surge of compassion, so quickly raised in him, that made Bill so lovable a character, so warm and valued a friend. He was infuriating in many ways, often selfish and thoughtless, but his affections were genuine, spontaneous, and he acted on them. He felt now that Anne, was his property, and plainly she needed him to look after her.

As soon as they rose from the table he went to her side, and when the party broke up he drove the Colegates back to Charles Street, and Anne to her flat.

Michael Vanstone was relieved. Barham's behaviour had saved him some awkward moments. He drove Jennifer to the nurses' home, and told himself yet again that he must do something about her. But he could hardly tackle her immediately after enjoying her parents' hospitality, he decided.

Chapter 4

'Come along, I'll take you to lunch,' Bill said firmly to Anne at the close of the Foundation meeting. 'Get your things.' Obediently she did so, while he at her elbow hustled her along impatiently, leaving her no time to renew her make-up or do her hair. They were soon walking across the hall and out through the archway into the traffic of Southampton Row. 'Little place I know,' Bill muttered, and dived down Guildford Street.

The little place turned out to be a pub in a turning off Doughty Street, where they sat among the lawyers, advertising men and journalists, and ate astonishingly good roast lamb with redcurrant jelly, washed down with Scotch ale.

'Excellent place this,' Bill remarked comfortably. 'Food's good, and you never see a soul you know. Damned useful. Can talk.' He drank ale and downed the lamb contentedly.

Bill enjoyed his food, and liked to dwell on it. His attitude, Anne thought, was entirely different from Michael's. He, for instance, if he said, 'a little place I know' would mean some quietly expensive restaurant tucked away in Soho or Knightsbridge, where the service would be smooth and the food exotic. Michael loved to discover restaurants where they did paella extraordinarily well, or where you could be sure of finding out-of-the-way shellfish, or other traveller's delights. Anne had, with him, consumed octopus in Frith Street, smorgasbord in Hanover Square, and fondue in Kensington High Street. Bill's idea of good food, on the contrary, was very English. City lunch places and steak houses were his choice and he seldom worried about whether the service was smooth or not. In fact, he would tolerate a surprising degree of matiness on the part of waiters, if the food pleased him.

'Very good roasts they do here,' he now announced, replete and agreeable, leaning back in his chair. 'Cheese now? Don't recommend anything else, their puddings are terrible. But their English cheese is reliable. They have a very nice Caerphilly, usually, and a good Double Gloucester. I wouldn't have the Roquefort, it's probably Danish Blue. Pity it's a bit early in the year for celery. Got to have frost on it. You look nice,' he added in congratulatory tones of some surprise. Now that his stomach was satisfied, Anne surmised, he had leisure to observe his environment, of which she formed part. 'That suit's a success. Hair looks different, too. I like it.'

Anne crinkled her eyes at him and smiled a little quizzically. This was the first occasion on which he had appeared to recognise her new flopping hair style. The suit that he liked had one of the newest scoop fronts, worn with a pleated blouse, that were all the rage that year. Her stepmother had fallen for it, and had insisted on buying herself a similar suit.

Pamela Colegate relied on Anne for what she considered to be fashionable London advice on clothes – she felt herself to be dowdy. Here she was correct. She was one of those tall, big-boned Australian women who have the knack of making their clothes look as if they belonged to someone else. She was at her best in slacks and shirts. She walked as though she were on a sheep station (which was not where she had been brought up), and strode through urban life like a well-meaning Labrador on the loose – amiable, inquisitive and over-exuberant. When she took Anne's advice on clothes she chose well. The trouble began when she followed not Anne's advice but her example. As for instance this scoop-fronted suit. This had been a disaster – remained a disaster, since Pamela Colegate was delighted with it, and considered it suited her wonderfully. Anne's was black, worn with a cinnamon blouse. Her stepmother had thought this colouring dull. 'A little dr-a-ab, dear?' Her suit was royal blue, with a puce blouse, not pleated but frilled. The effect was to say the least startling, but might have been success-ful on a very young girl. Style and colour combined to make Pamela Colegate look like the games mistress ineffectively dressed to play a barmaid in the staff play. If she sat quietly in it she was alarming enough, when she moved she was a riot.

Anne sighed now, and said, 'Well, yes, I was pleased with it. The trouble is, Pamela liked it, and she's bought herself the same sort of thing, and it isn't really *her* at all. Especially not in blue and puce.'

'Ah, I must have seen her in it, I think. She looked terrible. Poor Pamela. A good, kind soul – but people can't help laughing at her, poor dear. I thought she looked like a kindly Suffolk Punch got up for the Lord Mayor's show.'

It was true that no fashion succeeded in hiding Lady Colegate's sterling good-heartedness, though it was also possible for discerning onlookers to spot in her the early onset of the true battleaxe, and see her kinship with Lady Ramsay, twenty years older and tougher.

'She'll turn out exactly like Isobel Ramsay,' Bill now asserted, their minds evidently having run in unison. 'Good-hearted and clumsy-footed, not giving a damn for anyone – except for Murray, bless her. A wife in a million, as long as he doesn't mind people laughing at her behind her back. I couldn't stand that,' he added forcefully, and gave Anne an angry glare that puzzled her. Surely he couldn't be going into one of his notable rages over Pamela? Apparently not because he was now talking about the Foundation meeting.

'Of course,' he was saying, 'I can see what Vanstone means about controlled trials and keeping senior staff in the big centres to teach. It all sounds very sensible and ethical here at home. All that's wrong with it is that it simply has no real meaning as far as Nyganda is concerned.'

He had said this at the meeting. He and Michael had been locked in argument.

Neither of them had won, since the argument was more in the nature of a rehearsal than the real thing, though Bill had, unusually for him, slipped in a telling but sour aside. 'Evidently,' he had remarked to Michael for everyone to hear, 'you are not the stuff missionaries are made of.' 'Good God, no,' Michael had agreed, appalled.

The crunch would come when they thrashed it out at the Medical Committee. When that time came, Anne thought, Michael would almost certainly win. His was the orthodox teaching hospital attitude. Bill would be too go-ahead, too slapdash, to achieve backing. She couldn't help feeling sorry about it. Of course she wanted Michael to have a brilliant career, to become Professor of Medicine at – would it be thirty-seven or thirty-eight? He was marked for fame and success, and she would be proud to see him attain it. At the same time, she would like Bill to have a chance to see some of his ideas come to fruition. He had such enthusiasm, he was so practical and down to earth. She was sure that his plans would work, if only someone would give him the opportunity to carry them out. But after the fiasco of the bribery, this was hardly likely. And still Bill didn't seem to understand the implica-

120

tions of this for his own future. At the meeting this morning he had made no attempt to cover up, or to excuse himself. He had simply, as on other occasions, roared with laughter, and blamed his Nygandan clerk, who had dealt with the applications while Bill himself had been touring. 'Blow me,' he had said, 'do you know what I discovered the wretched fellow had been up to? Flogging the application forms at so much apiece.' He had shaken with laughter. 'There was I, confidently saying I could leave everything to Mwanze, tremendously able fellow, I told people. Dear oh dear, able is the word, he made rings round me all right. What a fool he made me look.' He had stopped laughing abruptly. 'Well, now we have to sort it out, I'm afraid. As I see it, we have no alternative but to return all the fake students home with a flea in their ear. Apart from the fact that they're no use to us, we have to do it for the look of the thing. *Poor encourager les autres.* Got to show bribery doesn't pay. That those who bribed their way into a free passage over here to the vast admiration of all their loved ones are soon back home in disgrace.'

Anne couldn't help it. Her heart sank. The administrative complication of this plan – and who was going to handle it? Herself, she could see that clearly enough. It would have meant hell in the office at any time, and with Clare only interested in her marriage, it would be murder. Blast Bill. She was thankful to hear Mr Arblaster objecting.

'They've cost us around £200 each in fares. Surely it would be better to insist either on getting some work out of them, even if they aren't up to our usual standard, or else throw them out. This would place them on the labour market, and should bring them up against reality with a dull thud. Teach them a lesson.' He was the House Governor, and it was his duty to balance the books of the Foundation.

Uncle Alec, however, would have none of this plan. 'There's nothing some of them want more than to be allowed to find their own jobs, having had their fares paid,' he pointed out. 'And those who aren't capable of finding proper jobs, the real misfits, will be lost outside the hospital. God knows where they'd end up. They're our responsibility. It's our fault we let them fiddle their way over here. We must either look after them or send them home.'

Matron wouldn't have them on the wards, she said, any longer.

Deadlock.

So they had rehashed it all. The outcome was that each student was to sit an examination and have a special report from the ward sister. (None of the medical students were involved in the débâcle. For one thing, they came at a different time of year, and for another, Bill had supervised their selection himself.) Those who failed the examination (and Miss Glossop thought the number would be over half) would either be sent home or work as orderlies.

'Mrs Heseltine will arrange all the details,' Ramsay said confidently. 'You'll get a suitable examination paper set, won't you, Matron? And arrange for the ward reports, and so on? Mrs Heseltine will fix a room for them to sit the examination, and for the invigilation, and for their final disposal afterwards. That all right?'

'Quite all right,' Anne said politely, her heart in her boots. What an assignment. She felt heavy with responsibility. Bill, who saw this, had at that moment decided to take her out to lunch as soon as the meeting was over, to cheer her up. His notion of doing this was apparently to berate her for not having acted on her own initiative much earlier. 'You should have sent them all home,' he asserted.

'I should have *what?*' Anne asked, staggered.

'Sent them all home. Your responsibility.'

Her responsibility. The injustice of it. She opened her mouth in fury.

'I know I boobed,' he interrupted her, apparently reading her expression. 'But Muggins Barham having put his big foot right in it, your job was to clear up the mess.'

'Thank you,' she said sarcastically, wondering how she could convey to him the fact that her main object had been to cover up for him as long as she could, not blow the whole inglorious failure sky high at the first opportunity.

'I know you,' he was saying rudely. 'You were just sitting there pretending the situation didn't exist, and hoping that it would evaporate into thin air as long as you didn't look it straight in the eye. Always been your worst fault. And it's not as if you can't act perfectly capably once you do decide to make a move. The trouble is, you wait for someone to give you the word. It's time you got a self-starter, duckie. You're a big girl now.'

She stared at him uncomfortably. He was right.

'If Tim was alive now,' he said, seeing right

through to her most hidden trickle of thought, that she had hardly been aware of herself, 'he would expect you to be grown up. Not dependent on him for all decisions.'

This was true. Her eyes misted, as she thought of Tim's absence over the past years, and the difference it had made to her. Since his death she had slipped into mediocrity, because there was no one to rally her.

Bill saw she had lapsed into remembrance, and dealt with this harshly. 'He would be disgusted to look at you and see you trying to find excuses to avoid the responsibilities of adult life.'

She hated him. 'You are being unfair and horrible,' she muttered.

'Not unfair. Horrible, yes. Got to jerk you into realisation. Look, let's get back to the job. Now, it's not enough to carry out the administration and the clerical work, and go round defending the students when they get into trouble, trying to persuade people to give them another chance. You've got take charge more than that. You've got to foresee the trouble, *you* must control *them*, not let them control you. You must have enough confidence to tick them off when they're in the wrong, to get in *before* other people, and *prevent* the poor saps from making fools of themselves. Not sit in your office waiting to mop up.'

'But Bill, you don't understand...'

'What don't I understand?'

'It's not right, it's never right, to force people along the road you decide they should take. They've got to find their own road, and take that, for their own reasons.'

'Of course, of course. I'm assuming you've enough intelligence to find out which is the right road. Your intelligence is perfectly adequate. What I'm saying is that you ought to have more decision. All overseas students lack confidence. They want you to have plenty of it. It reassures them. They feel they've found a competent guide in this bewildering new world. But if you are too insecure, they immediately go to pieces. For some reason that I've never quite been able to fathom, insecurity makes people play up like merry hell. Creates havoc all round. I've seen the results often enough to know exactly how to deal with it, though. It always works. You have to be on top of things all the time. That's all.'

Anne couldn't help breaking into laughter. Dear Bill, he advanced this solution as though anyone in the world could achieve it. Certainly, this was how he himself moved through life, making his mistakes as he went, but not worrying overmuch.

'It'll come with practice,' he now assured her. *'C'est le premier pas...'*

Anne sighed.

'When I got you this job I knew it would grow,' he stated. 'I was sure you would grow with it.' He looked at his watch. 'Better be getting back,' he remarked, and beckoned the waiter.

'Thank you for a lovely relaxing lunch,' Anne said glumly.

Bill, not at all put out, roared with laughter, and pulled her hair. 'Go to it, gal,' he said.

The thing about Bill was that after he had been talking, she did feel capable of almost anything. Somehow he had given her enormous self-confidence. She could go back to the office and do all he said and more.

It was just as well she felt this, as there was a fair amount to be done. The committee in the morning had not only decided to send the useless students home to Nyganda, but had also passed Miss Glossop's scheme for a preliminary training school there. Miss Glossop was to visit Ikerobe, accompanied by a nursing sister who would become matron of the school, and also accompanied (this, needless to say, engineered by Bill) by Clare, who would be the locally-based secretary and run the administration, with the aid of Nygandan girls. Anne would deal with it at the London end.

Bill had fought a battle on Clare's behalf. The Foundation thought her too young to take the responsibility of the new post. Bill had vouched for her capability and integrity, and had pointed out, rightly, that there was no one else to send. Miss Glossop could not spare her own secretary, Anne was needed at the London end. None of the medical secretaries had any experience in student administration. Far better, he argued, to send someone who already knew the scheme in all its intricacies. Any new secretary, however good her references and however senior her status, would be an unknown quantity. 'Anyway, Matron will be sending an experienced sister with her,' he had ended, and that had clinched it.

He had chuckled, as he and Anne had walked along Guilford Street together, and remarked, 'Now it only remains to see that Onajianya has such a good offer that he can't leave London for a couple of years. After that they can work it out for themselves.'

So now to tell Clare, Anne thought. When

she walked into her office, Clare was typing furiously – presumably in an effort to make up for lost time. She looked up briefly. 'Matron's been ringing you,' she said. 'But she's gone down to the annexe now. She said it would have to wait until tomorrow.'

'Thank heavens for that.'

'And Uncle Alec looked in and said if you needed him he'd be at Wimpole Street from half-past three onwards, and you could pop along for a cup of tea.'

Ann was full of roast lamb and Scotch ale, and felt in no need of tea. But the kindly summons could not be ignored. 'I'll go along,' she said. 'Can you find out from Mrs Fairfax how late I can leave it.'

She sighed. She was exhausted. She left Clare to the telephoning and went along to the cloakroom, where she washed vigorously, put on fresh make-up, re-did her eyes, combed out her hair and sprayed it. She drew a deep breath of relief. She felt better, clean and tidy and able to face the world. 'You'll do for another few hours,' she told her reflection. 'Now for Clare.' She went back to the office.

'Mrs Fairfax said tea will be at four-fifteen, and he's expecting you then.'

'Right. That gives me an hour before I

need go. Now, first of all, Bill Barham's fixed a job for you in Ikerobe.'

'What?' Clare breathed, her eyes lighting up.

'Yes. The training school plan is on, Matron's got it through at last. She's going out for a visit to prospect, taking a sister with her who'll run the school. You're to go too and run the scheme at that end – that's if you want to, and I suppose you do?'

'Too right I do,' Clare said, shining-faced. She had picked this expression up from Murray Colegate, and was at present working it to death. 'I never thought I had the slightest chance.'

'No, well, I didn't either, otherwise I would have mentioned it before the meeting. But Bill talked them into it, so you've got him to thank.'

'Oh, I do think he's *marvellous.*'

Anne smiled.

'Well, don't you?' Clare demanded. 'I don't mean just fixing this for me. I mean the way he gets things done, and the absolutely fantastic knack he has of always knowing exactly what needs doing.'

'Bill has always been a great getter of things done,' Anne agreed. She couldn't help it, the phrase came out rather acidly.

This was not only because she still smarted from his attack during lunch, but also because she could hardly fail to reflect that Clare would be less grateful if she knew what Bill was proposing to turn his hand to next – the retention of Onajianya in the United Kingdom.

'You don't appreciate him,' Clare said warmly. 'He's worth two of Michael Vanstone. I simply can't understand why you can't see it.' She then blushed a fiery pink, and began typing fast.

Anne blushed too, to her annoyance. 'He's quite different,' she said evasively, and changed the subject. 'Listen, we've got to get organised to send half the students home to Nyganda.' She told Clare what was involved. 'We can't get cracking until I've spoken to Matron, but we'd better clear the decks of everything else. Then I shall want someone in your place, and another girl to handle the Ikerobe training school stuff.' She looked at her watch. 'I've just time to ring the agencies before I go to see Uncle Alec. If they ring back you can make appointments. I'll have to see them at lunch time, I suppose, they always seem to want that. Try and keep them off Tuesday, though. I promised Pamela faithfully I'd meet her then for that foul fashion show. She's dying to see it, and honestly, I think she's dead scared of going alone.'

'I'm always willing to stand in for you,' Clare said with a gleam. She was back on to her old form already, Anne realised. 'Will you sign your letters while you're telephoning?' she went on.

'M-hm,' Anne agreed absently, and they appeared in front of her. She began talking to the first agency. 'Yes, with medical experience,' she said. 'Yes, any age between about twenty-two and fifty, I should think ... adaptable ... practical ... initiative ... mustn't mind pressure ... sense of humour... I'm afraid we can't possibly pay more ... oh, yes, good shorthand is absolutely essential.' She put the telephone down and frowned.

'Am I all that?' Clare asked with a pleased grin.

'You know you are – when you give your mind to it,' she added hastily. 'Anyway, you should have heard Bill. Anyone'd have thought you were a "top secretary". So you'd better keep it up when you get to Ikerobe.'

'It's all your doing, really,' Clare said, blushing furiously. 'I don't know how to tell you how grateful I am. You can't think what a difference it'll make – to have my own job, and a decent one. I shan't – I shan't be so committed,' she said in a rush. 'It – it isn't that I'm – I'm not going through with it or anything like that. Don't think that for a moment. I want to marry Onajianya. It's just that – that I was beginning to feel stampeded, that everything was going too fast for me.' She put her hands on top of the typewriter and clenched and unclenched them, frowning and pink still in the face.

Anne wished she had time to talk to her. Now she would have poured it all out, and Anne could have helped her to plan the future. But it was already after four, and she would be late for her appointment with Ramsay unless she left at once.

'We must have a proper talk,' she said firmly. 'Come and have supper – oh, blow. Not tonight. Um – well – I must fly – we'll fix something tomorrow.' She remembered that she had to meet the Colegates at Charles Street at six o'clock for drinks, and then Michael and the Taussigs were joining them for dinner. Her father knew Meg, of course, from her childhood, and he had firmly an-nounced that he was keeping an evening free 'of all these stuffed shirts I have to hobnob with now, and you get Meg along with that husband of hers and that boy friend of your own, and Pam and I'll have an evening off duty – go ahead and fix it, Anna-Maria.'

No one but Murray Colegate called Anne by this name. She had been christened Anne-Marie, her mother at that time going through a period of strong attraction towards anything continental, considering the name both pretty and 'different'. Murray had thought it affected, and had announced at the time that as far as he was concerned the poor little beggar would be Anne. In fact he had drifted into calling her Anna-Maria. As a child, Anne had hated and resented this form of her name, and at school she had concealed it. Now, in adult life, its use recalled memories of her childhood and old, enduring affections. Her heart warmed whenever she heard Murray's Australian twanging Anna-Mar-*rye*-a.

'Well, Anna-Maria,' he said to her when she arrived this evening, 'you're looking very smart and up-to-the-minute.'

'Up-to-the-minute,' Anne repeated. 'A good deal too much up-to-the-minute. Phoo!' She blew out dramatically and sank back into her chair, stretching her long legs before her. 'One of those days, I've had,' she announced.

'Then you need a stiff whisky,' Colegate said, and ordered it. 'Pam'll be down soon. When are these types arriving?'

'I told them sevenish.'

'Tell me about Michael Vanstone. He's the individual I keep meeting, who they're tipping for the Chair when Alec retires. Smooth type, intellectual?'

'That's him,' Anne said cautiously.

'A-ow,' her father said, exaggerating his Australian vowels. He looked at her, saw her closed, tense expression, and decided to say no more at present. The child looked as if she'd had enough, one way and another. 'How's Meg?' he enquired.

'She's fine. They've got this smashing new house, you know, and she's stopped working.'

'About time. Is this husband of hers any good?'

'Well, it's difficult to say. Andy's weird, of course, I simply don't know.' She began to tell her father about Meg and Andy's marriage, and how people were always foretelling its imminent break-up. 'Michael says–' she began, when they were interrupted by the arrival of Pamela. She was wearing the blue and puce abomination, and she and Anne at once dissolved into giggles and pointed quivering fingers at each other.

'Snap,' Pamela said. 'Wouldn't you *know* we'd both have to wear it. I'm damned if I'm going to climb back upstairs and change.'

'Whatever for?' Colegate asked lazily. 'No one'll notice. You don't look in the least alike,' he added with truth but little tact.

'Naow,' Pamela agreed. 'That's just what I'm afraid is painfully obvious. No good me making any attempt to look like this beautiful daughter of yours.'

'You look OK,' her husband replied comfortably.

'Gee, thanks, dear, you overwhelm me,' Pamela said sarcastically.

At this point Andy and Meg arrived, and shortly afterwards Michael. There were introductions and more drinks were ordered. Anne was amused to notice that both Andy and Michael were on their best behaviour, very correct, very formal. She commented on this after dinner to Meg, when they were sharing a sofa in the drawing-room and drinking coffee. Meg giggled. 'I know,' she said. 'It's rather sweet, isn't it? Uncle Murray's a great man now, the pet, and boy, do they know it?'

'Dear old Dad,' Anne said affectionately. 'He's become terribly important. I can't get over it. Pam's got a mink, would you believe it? Hideously unbecoming, which seems a pity. I tried it on. It was still hideous on me – a great ballooning thing with vast cuffs – but I must admit it felt good.'

'In the mink,' Meg said dreamily. 'One thing I can be dead certain I shall never be. Oh well. How's the hospital? What's cooking?'

'We had the Foundation meeting this morning, you know. Bill fixed it for Clare to go out to Nyganda to run the scheme from that end – see there's no more bribery, I suppose,' she added tartly. She had not yet forgiven Bill for disturbing her so much.

'Good for him. I do think he's a sweetie, the way he looks after everyone. If only he'd spare the occasional moment to look after himself, he wouldn't get into these awful muddles.'

'And now he's organising Onajianya into staying here a bit longer.'

'That won't please either of them, of course. But they'll have to lump it, and it'll give Clare a breathing space, and a bit of time to find out what she really thinks of the country. Of course, Onajinaya is tremendously attractive, no doubt about that. I quite see why she wants to take him on. And she must feel so adventurous and pioneering at the same time.' Meg sounded almost envious.

'Then they've passed Matron's training school in Ikerobe – she's off next month on a preliminary canter.'

'That'll please the old war horse. So she's got it through at last, has she? I never really thought she'd manage it. Lord, how everything's changing since I left.' Her tones were regretful, and she drank coffee abstractedly.

The men were sitting over brandy in the bar, and Pamela had gone to her bedroom to fetch 'a little clothes brush I bought in Harrods this morning, called "baby boffin", and I tried it on Murray's dark suit and it really worked. You must both get one.' Pamela always shared her discoveries with the world. She came in now, waving the small brush. 'Here it is,' she announced unnecessarily. She looked round. 'Nothing to try it on, here,' she said, disappointed. Anne was relieved. She had feared Lady Colegate would march up to the two elderly men sitting on the other side of the room and insist on demonstrating the baby boffin on their suits. 'Now,' she went on, 'I want to hear all about your new house, Meg. Tell me.'

'Um,' Meg said. 'It's modern.'

'Anne told me that much,' Pamela retorted. 'Describe it.'

'Well,' Meg hesitated. 'The trouble is,' she went on in a rush, 'I don't much like it.'

'You don't *like* it?' Anne repeated. 'What on earth's wrong with it? When I think of your terrible old flat. Honestly. Anyway, the house is simply fabulous, I should have thought. *Honestly.*'

Meg wriggled. 'It's fabulous for holding parties in,' she said flatly. 'Perhaps that's what's wrong with it. It doesn't feel like home. More like a corner of the Festival Hall. I keep waiting for when it'll be time to leave and go home. But there's nowhere to go.'

'I know just what you mean, dear,' Pamela said. 'Not cosy, eh? What you want is a coupla kids.'

Anne was silent. The conversation seemed to be running away with itself.

'I don't want a couple of kids,' Meg said forcefully. 'What would I do with a couple more like Andy underfoot?'

Anne opened her mouth, but Pamela forestalled her. 'Of course, I know *exactly* what you mean,' she said. 'But they might be like you, or your side of the family, anyway.'

'And a dead bore that would be,' Meg

asserted snappily. Evidently nothing suited her at present. She returned to the house, and continued to complain about it. 'No one could possibly imagine bringing up children in *that* place. It's like that song of Michael Flanders, terribly H and G. "The gardens' full of furniture and the house is full of plants". And I never want to see another piece of teak again as long as I live.'

'But Meg,' wailed Anne, 'I think it's simply gorgeous. What's the *matter* with you?'

'I don't know what's the matter with me,' she admitted. 'Boredom, probably. For years I thought that leisure was the most precious possession anyone could have – only I never managed to have it. Now I've got it, lashings of it, and all I notice is that *nothing*, absolutely *nothing*, happens between one meal and the next.'

'I felt exactly the same when I stopped working,' Pamela agreed. 'What you need is a family. Otherwise it's hell being at home. Of course, once you've got them, it's hell with them and the blasted patter of those flipping tiny feet, not to mention the tiny voices deafening you. But by then it's too late, you can't do without the little horrors. Of course, when Murray comes home, it's all right.'

Anne wondered if Meg would say, 'Well, when Andy comes home it isn't all right.'

Whether she would have confided this they were not to know, as the men reappeared, and Pamela at once brandished her little brush at them. 'Now I can show the girls,' she exclaimed with satisfaction. 'Come here, Murray, and let me show them how beautifully – oh, you're no good, not a speck to be seen. Let's look at you,' she said, seizing on Michael, whose face took on an expression of utter astonishment that convulsed Meg. 'No good either,' she stated. 'What about you?' advancing on Andy. 'Ah, that's more like it. Covered in scurf,' she said in ringing tones. 'Now then, girls, look here.'

'What a very alarming woman your step-mother is,' Michael remarked cautiously, as he drove Anne back to her flat later.

'Oh, she's rather a dear,' Anne said comfortably.

'I thought she was quite horrific,' Michael said. In spite of this, however, he was becoming more and more determined to attach himself permanently to Anne. Thank God, though, that Pamela Colegate would be half a world away.

The more he thought about the situation

141

he was in, the more certain he became that his love for Anne was real and his affair with Jennifer false. Since his moment of clarity when Ramsay had first mentioned Murray Colegate's name at the Foundation meeting, he had not attempted to deceive himself. He had become accidentally involved with Jennifer, and nothing but his own feebleness and anxiety not to offend Ramsay was preventing him from extricating himself. Until he ended the present situation with Jennifer he could not ask Anne to marry him. And this, he had decided, was what he wanted.

He left her at her flat now, not lingering as she had expected him to do, but going off to Wimpole Street determined to tell Jennifer that their affair must end. 'And be blowed to the Chair,' he announced to the bathroom mirror. 'I want it. I want it badly. But not at that price.'

In any case, an inner voice suggested, Uncle Alec was not the sort of man to penalise him simply because he failed to marry his daughter. Or so he hoped.

Chapter 5

Anne was eating sandwiches at her desk, and cogitating on the candidates for Clare's job whom she had interviewed, when Clare came bursting in. 'Isn't it *fantastic* about Meg Taussig?' she exclaimed. 'I must say, I'm absolutely delighted. I can't think of *any* of the sisters I'd rather be working with. But all the same, of course I can see that if it means–'

'What are you talking about? What about Meg?'

'Haven't you heard?'

'Heard what? I haven't heard anything about Meg.'

'Do you mean to say you didn't know she's to be matron of the Ikerobe training school?'

'*What?*'

'It's definite. The whole place is seething with it. It never occurred to me that you didn't know. I thought she'd have been sure to tell you about it herself. They are all saying it's the final break-up of that marriage. No one can talk about anything else. Of course, you've been so busy interviewing and so on,

I don't suppose you've so much as stepped outside this room yesterday or today but if you had you'd have been sure to hear–'

'How long's she going for?'

'Permanently, everyone says. Of course, she's just going out for the preliminary visit with Matron next month, but apparently she's definitely been appointed as matron of the training hospital. The idea seems to be that we shall both of us practically commute between here and Nyganda to begin with (the Foundation seems very flush with money and fares, all off a sudden, I must say) but that pretty soon we'll both be there all the time. She's going to have some junior sisters from here, and Nygandan staff nurses who trained here. But of course you know all this.'

'Only part of it,' Anne said. 'Some of it is what Matron and I discussed yesterday morning. But she seems to have gone a good deal further since then with her plans. Anyway she never mentioned Meg – I feel sure she would have done.'

'Oh surely,' Clare agreed. 'Actually–'

'I must say we spent most of our time planning the examination, and what we'd do with the failures. I didn't have time to tell you before, but in the end, we came to the con-

144

clusion that instead of sending them home in complete disgrace, if they really want to nurse, they can go back to Nyganda and be among the first entrants to the new school. Then it won't matter if they aren't up to Central standards, and they can go back to square one and take their time. So now they'll be Meg's pigeon. Blow me. I do think she might have told me she intended to do this.'

'She saw Matron yesterday afternoon.'

'Did she? She might have looked in here on her way out. Blast her, I'm going to find out what she's been up to.' Anne picked up her telephone and asked for a line. 'Meg? What's all this? The whole hospital's talking about you and saying you're off to Nyganda any moment now.'

'As a matter of fact, I am,' Meg's voice replied calmly, happily, it seemed. 'Sorry I didn't tell you before, but it all happened in such a rush, once I'd made up my mind.'

'Oh, don't mention it. I can pick it up around the place as long as I keep my ears flapping.'

'I was going to ring you anyway,' Meg was undisturbed. Anne had never in all their long friendship been able to panic her. 'I would have come in to see you yesterday, after I'd

145

seen Matron, but I thought I'd better tell Andy first, or there'd be real trouble.'

'Do you mean to say you didn't discuss it with him?'

'No, I just made up my mind – after you told me about the training school that evening, in fact. It came like a solution to everything, handed to me on a plate. So I rang up Matron, and she said to come and see her, and that was that.'

'What does Andy say?'

'As a matter of fact he's livid.'

'He minds, then?'

'I don't know whether he *minds,* or whether he's simply furious with me for being independent. Look, come and have supper this evening – he said he wouldn't be in, he went off very grand and uffish this morning, saying he wouldn't trouble me to get any more meals for him, he'd eat out. So you come here, and we can have a good talk.'

Anne agreed to this. There was certainly plenty to talk about.

'He got drunk last night,' Meg told her when she arrived at the Hampstead house. 'So that was very helpful. Then this morning, as I said, he was all grand and distant. I think he had a terrible hangover, poor lamb. So we haven't got down to discussing it. But of course I can tell, and he's absolutely furious with me.'

'Has he asked you not to go?'

'Oh no. He wouldn't demean himself. He's merely abused me. Told me what a fool I am. I must be round the bend. All women are impossible but I'm more impossible than most, that sort of thing. I must say I see what he means. I am being rather impossible, but I can't help it. The alternative would be to turn into one of those ghastly empty-headed women who can do nothing but drift about and go shopping.'

'You could never be a bit like that.'

'Oh couldn't I? That's what you think. I'm rapidly turning into one, I can tell you – mooning about my luxurious house and grumbling, my only diversion to go to Heal's and look at curtain materials. Andy's furious with me about the house. He accuses me of refusing to accept anything from him – he says he let me give him his medical training, but I won't let him give me a house. I hadn't the heart to point out that we bought the house with my shares – I thought that would be the last straw as far as he was concerned. He's got it all worked out. He says I'm indulging in a sort of one-upmanship, that I'm not prepared to be on the receiving end myself. I can give to him, and feel smug, he says, but now it's his turn to do the giving, I can't take with a good grace. Another thing he's livid about is that he says I made him watch me working hard and feel guilty about it, but now he's giving me leisure I won't accept that either. He says I'm neurotically determined to reject him and anything he offers, and he wouldn't mind so much if only I'd be straightforward about it, instead of saying there's a need in Nyganda.'

'I must say – it's not that I want to criticise, don't get me wrong, I'm only *asking* – but why Nyganda? I mean, if it's idleness and emptiness that's getting you down, why not just go back to nursing at the Central? Why rush off to Nyganda?'

'There you are,' Meg cried triumphantly. 'That's Andy's point. And that's what I *said*. I'm being irrational and neurotic, I'm driven, I can't help myself, it's compulsive. Andy's perfectly right, I'm being *impossible*, I know what you both say is sensible. The way to go about this is gradually, feeling my way and finding out what I really want, and what's best to do. But I can't be sensible. I've got to break out and put physical distance between me and Andy.'

'That sounds,' Anne said bluntly, 'as if you don't really want to leave him. As if you aren't sure about it yet.'

'Of course I'm not sure. How could I be? I've been married to him for ten years. A third of my life. I can't imagine what life will be like without him. I can't bear the idea of leaving him, that's the truth. Of not having him with me, of not being able to look after him any more.' To Anne's astonishment, her lips quivered and her eyes filled and spilled over. She pulled out her handkerchief irritably and blew her nose loudly. 'But I can't go on like this either.'

'I still don't understand why not a job at the Central.'

'I expect it's because I want to hurt Andy,' Meg said in a dead voice. 'I want to deal him a mortal blow, and then go away somewhere else so that I don't have to stay and see the consequences.'

Anne found that the situation had gone beyond her. She could not any longer understand what Meg was talking about. She looked helplessly at her.

'Before I go,' Meg said briskly, 'what about you and Michael?'

'Oh God, I don't know,' Anne said. She was astonished to hear herself. What didn't she know. She had thought herself to be happy with Michael. What could she be meaning?

'You don't know about him any more than I know about Andy,' Meg pointed out. 'You know, I'm afraid neither of us is very good at picking our men.'

Anne was indignant. How could Meg compare Michael, so successful, brilliant, gentle and considerate (not to mention – she was horrified to find herself thinking this, and pushed the embarrassing thought away, but there was no doubt that it had entered her head – genuine British upper-middle class instead of an Austrian nobody) with the impossible Andy?

'He's always been one to blow hot and cold for no apparent reason,' Meg was continuing. She was trying to cushion Anne against the inevitable impact of discovering Michael's unfaithfulness. To her surprise. Anne did not defend him.

'I know,' she said. 'I keep asking myself can it possibly last? Wondering whether I was a complete fool to get involved with him. I'd vowed I wouldn't, you know. I'd told myself, after all those false starts, that I wouldn't ever again fall for one of his approaches. Then of course I did, because it seemed so inevitable. So much *meant*. Sometimes I think that all the time we *had* been meant for one another, and that there's nothing to worry about.'

'But you do worry?' Meg asked quickly.

'Yes, I do worry. But it's partly just me, you know.' She hesitated. 'I do always find it immensely difficult to begin to trust anyone with my true feelings. I've hardly ever talked, really talked, to anyone except you and Tim. Not even to Dad. Of course, that's partly because of boarding school and not having a home.'

'And because of not having a mother,' Meg said firmly. 'You may row with your mother, you may end up by despising her, as I half do mine, but you can always talk to her if you want to. Usually you don't want to, because you've found other people to talk to – but you do your learning on her. It's been very hard on you, your mother dying when you were so young.'

'Well, I had Dad,' Anne said, feeling she had been disloyal to him. 'But I think I admired him too much to do anything but try to put my best side forward. Tim's the only person who I ever felt sure would take me as I am – oh, and I suppose Bill. You always feel sure Bill wouldn't care how

151

awful you were. Of course, I have talked to *him,* too. He forces me to by making me annoyed, and I blurt everything out.' She paused, plaiting her long fingers. Meg said nothing. 'I think, you see,' she finally went on, 'that all my worry about Michael may be just that – that I can't quite get to the point of trusting him, because I don't, really, trust anybody. I wish I did.'

At that moment Meg saw why Bill had been so angry to hear that Michael was making a fool of Anne. She was angry herself now, and further away than ever from telling Anne the truth about Michael and Jennifer. How could she?

'You see,' Anne was saying, 'if that's all my worry is – just me, teetering on the brink as usual – the sooner I get over it the better. I'm just spoiling things for myself, that's all. I don't know,' she said, 'if only one could be sure of people, instead of all mixed up.'

Meg smiled brilliantly, and sadly. 'We're just a couple of mixed-up kids, in fact,' she stated.

She was thinking now of Andy. Although she had dreaded his return from Nyganda, had been determined to break with him finally, as soon as he was back in reality she found herself to be far more deeply committed to him than she had realised. Their physical love was still strong and satisfactory, and she was fighting her own instincts as she prepared to leave him. He had bruised her spirit, which cried out to be free of him. But her body still craved the comfort of his flesh and protested vehemently, unmistakably, that it needed him. And Andy needed her, there was no doubt about that. He had returned to her not only with passion but also with devotion, like a child to its mother. She had welcomed him physically with excitement and tenderness, and after making love they lay together in peace and surety, their quarrels forgotten. The comfort of their close and loving warmth made a mockery of her plan to leave him. How could she go? To leave Andy would be to tear wantonly apart a single living organism. Neither of them could survive it. She could not do it.

Yet as the days went by she knew she was going to do it. Life without Andy would be empty, but with him it was vicious. To separate from him would be to leave part of herself behind, and to carry part of him with her wherever she went. But to stay was impossible. She had no further strength for it. She could see, too, that it was futile to continue to spoil her life for him. 'The trouble, is,' she said to Anne, 'that I don't believe in him any longer. I can't understand why I ever did. I was just bamboozling myself. It wasn't even his doing. He never pretended to me. I must be fair, he always told me he was nasty. I just chose not to believe him. I suppose I was young and romantic, and saw only what I wanted to see. Now I can see clearly. He is nasty.'

This was what everyone had said all along, Anne reflected. But Meg still had to come to it the hard way. The bitter way of experience. 'No one can live life for us,' she said. 'Taking advice is no help. We still have to live through events for ourselves, or remain immature children for ever. Perhaps maturity is worth gaining? Perhaps when it's attained it's comfortable? Worthwhile?'

'I wouldn't know,' Meg retorted. 'And I rather despair of finding out. All I've learnt is that love is bloody difficult, like moving blindfold towards someone who can't speak your language. You clasp hands and you're afraid to let go, but you still can't see anything but darkness or hear sounds that you recognise. You think it might be only sensible to let go, and you'd meet someone whom you could understand. And who would understand you. But then you notice that no one else can even succeed in catching the hand of anyone, they're all alone, and you think that you have something most people never find, as they stand shouting unintelligibly across vacancy.'

'Do you honestly think it's as difficult as that?' Anne asked, appalled at the strain of the relationship Meg had revealed. Did Meg think this was what all marriages were like?

'Yes,' Meg said forthrightly. Could Anne have forgotten what it had been like when Tim was alive, she wondered? They had been in touch, and the result had not always been comfortable for either of them. But Anne seemed now not to know what she was talking about. 'Most people,' she reiterated, trying to make Anne remember, 'most people have only easy superficial associations with others. Quite companionable and useful. I'm as sociable as anyone.'

This was true, Anne knew. She considered it made what Andy had done to Meg even worse. Meg was exceptionally easy to get on with.

'But sociability and companionship are nothing to do with fusion. That's when all the difficulties start – and life is worth living,' she added with a sigh. 'I wish I knew what to do.' She shook herself vigorously, like a dog coming out of water, and stated curtly, 'Well, I do know what to do. I'm going to Nyganda, and that's that. I shall probably never come back to Andy, or to this house.' She gave it an evil look. 'It may have been worth while putting Andy through medicine, I don't know. But making him the centre of my life now is just plain silly. I'm not going to do it any longer. He can look after himself.'

Anne found all this unbearably depressing, and turned to Michael for comfort. 'I'm dreadfully unhappy about Meg and Andy's break-up,' she began.

'Good God, why on earth?' he asked, surprised. 'We've all seen it coming for years. It's been inevitable. Good thing it's happened at last, I should have thought. No point in them going on. Nothing to get worked up about in that.'

'Meg's so dreadfully unhappy.'

'I daresay she is. But she's got to make the break sometimes. It was bound to happen.' He shrugged in a way he had, which meant, *c'est la vie*'. Ann could have hit him. How dared he simply shrug off all that pain? To be so totally uninvolved was callous. To change the subject, as agreement was obviously impossible while they talked about Meg, she began to discuss the future of the training hospital, and what could be made of it.

Michael shrugged again. 'It seems to me that everyone at the Central has become obsessed with Africa. Personally, I think the importance of Nyganda, in particular, is greatly overrated.'

This was as much treason to Anne as it would have been to Ramsay himself. All her frustration, her irritation with Michael, her unhappiness over Meg, were flung into the ensuing quarrel.

Michael had a prosperous business family background, and had been brought up to think the Commonwealth an outmoded sentimentality, a Kiplingesque affectation. No clear-thinking man, he had decided, in adult life, could fall for such muddle-headed nonsense. He told Anne this, and she was shocked to her core. She could not grasp how he could be blind to this reality of brotherhood, which to her was so much more than a vision or an ideal. It was based firmly in her own family history and her present daily work. The Commonwealth, she told him, was far more real than any woolly-minded notions of the Common Market, based on trade interests alone. This, she told Michael succinctly, would fall apart at the seams the moment it failed to bring material prosperity. 'After all, what is there to hold it together? Not even a common language.'

Michael laughed scornfully. 'It's time the English grew out of this lazy habit of never bothering to learn any other language than their own,' he retorted. He was fluent in French and German, and had a smattering of Dutch. He could usually make himself understood anywhere in Europe. Anne knew this, of course, and she abandoned the Commonwealth as a lost cause, and turned to Africa, speaking of Ramsay's childhood there, and his ability to speak a number of Nygandan dialects.

'Much good it's done him,' Michael snapped.

'But that's not the point at all,' Anne said unhappily. There seemed to be an enormous chasm between them. Throughout this conversation their words had been far enough apart, but their hearts were completely out of touch. They had not, when it came to it, known what the other was talking about. So much for a common language. 'We just don't speak the same language,' she wailed, and was horrified to hear the truth spoken out like this. The truth? Could it be the truth? Surely not.

Michael was disconcerted. And irritated. Anne was picking a quarrel with him – about Nyganda, of all places. But he was damned if he would pretend to believe it important, just to humour her. He thought she was letting him down by being so disagreeable, scratchy and lacking in sympathy, when he was preparing to give up so much for her sake. Well, not exactly give up the Chair, after all. Or at least he hoped not. In any case, give up his opinions he would not.

'All this emphasis on what we can do for Nyganda is sentimental rubbish,' he said. 'In that sense I agree we don't speak the same language. I don't share your ideas about the importance of the blasted country, and I certainly don't intend to say I do, simply to placate you.'

'I'm not asking you to *placate* me,' Anne retorted. She sighed. They were drifting further apart with every sentence. They separated coldly, unlovingly. Afterwards Anne wept. What had made her quarrel with Michael, about Nyganda, of all strange choices? Did it matter? Did it have anything to do with their love? Surely not? She slept uneasily, and woke depressed.

Chapter 6

The hospital summer ball was a great occasion, dressed for with some ceremony. Jennifer had been planning what she would wear for weeks, and looked forward to shining before everyone as Michael's chosen girl friend. But the day before the ball he broke with her, told her their relationship had to end. It was not fair to her, he said.

'Surely I am the one to decide that?' Jennifer had answered calmly, though in fact she was terrified. Was he really going to leave her?

'You must find someone younger, more suited to you,' Michael said implacably. Now he had finally brought himself to the point, he was determined to go through with his severance, clearly, unmistakably, with no lingering half-measures. 'I'm just taking advantage of you, when you're too young to know what you want.'

'I do know what I want,' Jennifer said.

Michael ignored this inconvenient truth, and went on with his rehearsed speech.

'You're terribly sweet, and I love you dearly.'

So lightly said. Jennifer's stomach turned to ice, and began to radiate cold signals of despair.

'But I'm not the right man for you. You want to go about with some young man, who wants to settle down and raise a family.'

Jennifer was frozen now. Michael was going to tell her he had no intention of marrying her. Her world had no other meaning. She stared at him, silenced at last.

'I don't want to marry you.' Now he had said it. 'I have no right to amuse myself with you. You're so charming and difficult to resist – I should have said this before. I've been unfair to you.' He went on in this strain for some time, and then left her at the nurses' home. She had gone up to her room, almost stunned with disappointment, knowing that the pain would strike her soon. At once, when she opened the door of her room she saw her ball dress hanging on the cupboard door. She had ironed it yesterday, imagining herself at the ball with Michael. Surprisingly, what came immediately was not pain, but anger. How could he do this to her, just before the ball? The utter selfishness of it. Why couldn't he have waited just another day and escorted her to the ball as he had promised, so that everyone would see them together?

A second thought quickly followed. He would have to escort her, or else explain himself to her father. He would have to join them, he couldn't miss the ball. He could hardly excuse himself to her father and go alone. For years he had been included in their party.

Instead of despair, hope flickered. The next day, on the wards, she went about her duties as efficiently as usual. Occasionally fear swept her, but she pushed it aside. When the evening came, she dressed with anticipation. Surely when he saw her in this heavenly dress he would forget what he had said?

Lady Ramsay came up to the nurses' home to fetch her and to apply finishing touches. Thoughtfully, she had brought with her her own perfume, and Jennifer smothered herself in it. Lady Ramsay had also brought her diamond ear-rings, and Jennifer's own diamond pendant. She thought her daughter looked lovely, and had no inkling that anything might be wrong. And in her excitement, screwing the diamonds into her ears, fastening the pendant, spraying her hair, fiddling with her eye make-up, Jennifer herself forgot.

'I think I look rather nice,' she said smugly. 'Has Michael arrived?'

'I left him and your father, needless to say, propping up the bar,' Lady Ramsay said tolerantly. 'They seemed to consider they needed fortifying for the ordeal ahead.' She was astonished to see Jennifer shoot her a sudden anguished glance, and afterwards decided she must have imagined it. A trick of the light.

They went down together, Lady Ramsay stuffily prosperous in brown brocade with a heavy mink stole, and Jennifer a little like the fairy off the top of the Christmas tree, in pink chiffon, billowing out into a full skirt, the diamonds sparkling at her ears and throat. Flushed and young, she could get away with it – just. They arrived at the Great Hall at the same time as the Colegates, with Anne, and Bill Barham, who had all been dining together, and there were greetings and a flurry of activity, so that Michael's welcome to both Jennifer and Anne passed unnoticed except by the three concerned.

Anne was wearing a shot blue and green silk shift, liquid and shimmering, slim as a reed. Her blue eyes were shadowed with green and her blonde hair hung loose and straight. She was at her most sophisticated, she had an evening coat, long and straight also, to match the dress, and looked almost magical to Jennifer, who at once felt like a schoolgirl in her waisted dress with its full skirt.

The group was soon joined by Meg and Andy, who took all eyes and at once became the centre of speculation. Meg was unmistakably *en grand tenue*, in coral silk, glowing with vitality. It was apparent to anyone whose glance passed over them, even abstractedly, that Andy could not take his eyes off her, and that they were tied by an invisible but almost tangible web of desire. The two of them, bursting with overwhelming life (no one had ever suggested that Andy lacked virility, however much they might deprecate his behaviour) made Michael Vanstone seem more than usually intellectual and withdrawn. The hospital speculated happily whether Andy and Meg were reconciled and whether, accordingly, Matron would have to find a new candidate to run the Ikerobe hospital, and whether Michael Vanstone had quarrelled with both his girl friends, as he was clearly not partnering either of them – or whether he was merely terrified out of his wits. After all, he had, as a number of people took pleasure in pointing out to one another, not only to contend with Jennifer and Anne, one on each side of him, both dressed to kill, but with their respective fathers, each looking slightly larger than life and twice as influential.

In any case, Michael did his strict duty by Jennifer and Anne, but no more. He danced once with each of them, as against twice with Lady Ramsay and Lady Colegate. He managed to prise Meg away from Andy for a dance, he had a dance with Miss Glossop, and he went the rounds of his colleagues' wives and daughters, and fitted in a dance with Derek Wooldridge's girl friend, half-naked as usual, and Clare.

Bill Barham, normally more sociable than Michael, spent the evening within a much narrower circle, and danced mainly with Anne. This gave the hospital something new to talk about though in fact the two of them were involved in a prolonged discussion about Onajianya and Clare and the future of the new training hospital, which lasted, with interruptions, not only through half a dozen dances but also through supper. Bill thought he had been able to fix a job for Onajianya which would undoubtedly keep him in England for another two years, he announced. Meg, Anne was able to tell him, had promised to look after Clare in Nyganda – though would she still be going, Anne demanded in agitation, uncertain whether to be glad or sorry, as Meg swept by, radiant in Andy's arms.

'Ask her,' Bill said briefly.

Anne did so. 'Is it all on again between you and Andy? Are you not going to Nyganda after all?' she asked, when they returned to their table, and Bill took Andy with him in search of more champagne and more ice.

'Of course I am,' Meg said in apparent amazement. 'Why ever not?'

'Just – I thought – you see, I wondered if – I mean, you and Andy, honestly,' she finished in an embarrassed rush, 'after all, you look as if you've just this minute fallen in love.'

Meg sighed, and smiled with a heart-rending desolate beauty that stunned Anne in its tragic maturity. 'We are,' she said simply. 'We are. But we wouldn't be if I wasn't going away. So there it is. This is our Waterloo Ball. Our future is anyone's guess. But tonight – at least we have tonight, and each other. Or what passes for each other. Let's end with a bang not a whimper,' she held out her glass to Bill, returned with more champagne. 'Lashings of champagne, Bill darling, bless you,' she said, her eyes shining, 'think of me occasionally when I'm slaving away in Ikerobe.'

Bill laughed – or being Bill, he did more than laugh, he shook bodily with overpowering amusement. 'My dear girl, the way things are going I shan't be here in London swilling champagne and sparing you the occasional thought. I'm far more likely to be out in Nyganda sweltering in the bush while you luxuriate in the facilities of Ikerobe.'

'Are you going back to Nyganda?' both voices chorused in amazement.

'Don't you think it looks rather like it?' Bill asked. 'Muggins Barham has definitely blotted his copybook here in London, there won't be any distinguished post for *him* next autumn. That'll be kept for young don't-put-a-foot-wrong Vanstone. And there is a hell of a lot needing to be done in Nyganda. Come on, Anne, let's have another dance. I want to enjoy civilisation while I can.'

'Do you really mean it?' she asked. 'Are you seriously intending to go back to Nyganda? You've only just *done* a year there.' She sounded a little querulous, and, to her amazement, felt like bursting into tears. Was Bill going to desert her? Had he come back into her life only to leave it again? Clasped warmly against his bulky form as they danced, she felt momentarily that she could not bear to let him go.

When they returned to their table, they coincided with Ramsay and Miss Glossop, who had been dancing together. Miss Glossop was wearing a plain dark blue silk dress, which looked as if it only awaited the slipping on of her starched cuffs. 'It must have been made for her by Garroulds,' Meg whispered. These were the nursing uniform specialists. 'It's probably part of a line in "off-duty wear for teaching hospital matrons". Perhaps I'd better go and get something to wear at Ikerobe occasions.'

Murray Colegate had greeted Miss Glossop with champagne and a cry going back to the days when he had been a houseman and she a gangling staff nurse. 'Well, and how is Lord Glossop's girl today?' She grinned companionably back at him, while Anne and Meg caught one another's eyes in amazement. More was to come. There was a pause in the dancing, as the bands changed over, and the hubbub of talk rose high to the vaulted roof. It was at this moment that Pamela Colegate dropped a brick to rival any of Isobel Ramsay's. She could not quite place Matron, Lord Glossop's daughter apparently, she supposed she must be either a woman doctor – she looked as if she might be, too – or else perhaps the wife of one of the consultants. Or was Lord Glossop the Chairman of the Governors? In any case, she was obviously meant to know her, and she launched into laboured conversation with a cliché about 'so many people here tonight', rambled on vaguely for a sentence or two, and ended, before anyone realised what was coming, with 'the only person I don't seem to have met is Matron – just as well, I suppose, if she's like all the matrons I've ever come across, a ferocious old battle-axe.'

The remark lay in a thunderous silence, in which the hubbub surrounding them served only to emphasise the enormity of the irretrievable remark. The occasion was saved by Colegate himself, who smacked Miss Glossop on her well-covered behind with a report like a pistol shot – so that despite the parrot-house crescendo all heads turned – and remained turned, the sight of the Matron of the Central being resoundingly whacked on the bottom being distinctly unusual. 'Well,' Murray asked into the abrupt hush, his Australian accent more pronounced than ever, 'and what does Lord Glossop's girl have to say to that, you ferocious old whatnot?'

Miss Glossop was delighted, and turned a beaming face to him. 'You cheeky Aussie,' she said, 'grow up.'

The story lost nothing in the telling, and was to become incorporated, with embellishments, into hospital legend. 'You cheeky Aussie,' they were to remark in future to all their Australian visitors, '–what's good enough for Murray Colegate's good enough for you, isn't it? And by the way, when are you going to whack Matron? We're all waiting. You have to do it before you leave, you know – or else it's drinks all round.' Generations of Australians were to settle for drinks all round.

Pamela Colegate's face was red and sweating, and she looked unhappy and ashamed. Her evening was ruined, almost her whole trip spoilt for her. 'Oh dear,' she whispered to Ramsay, as soon as the conversations round about were under way again. 'I've let Murray down.' He saw she was miserable. 'My dear, don't think about it. Murray won't mind, so why should you? You're a good girl,' he said, patting her broad and muscular shoulder, 'and you've made him happy.' She murmured something about failing him always. 'Nonsense, my dear. I've known Murray for twenty years now. I knew him in his first marriage, and I knew him after Margaret's death. With you now he's content. No doubt about it.'

Pamela drank it in, as Ramsay had known she would. She had never been able to get over her luck in capturing Murray, and she had always known she was not good enough for him. Warm-hearted and outward-looking, she had tried to make him happy and to give him what he wanted in life. She had no self-importance, and she never expected to take the place of his first wife in his heart – or even of Anne, beautiful daughter of that sophisticated London marriage.

Her trouble was that she was right about this. Murray had married her because he wanted a wife and family, and someone to run his home for him. He had chosen Pamela because she was not only competent and eager to marry him, but because he judged that she was kind and fair, and would be a reliable partner. All this was cold blooded, and bore no likeness to his marriage with Margaret, who had often been difficult, but whom he had loved passionately. This early love he had kept intact in his memory, with his early life in London, when he had been untried, and the world had opened before him, exciting and full of hope. His beloved Anne now held first place in his romantic affections, while his second wife and family were part of everyday routine. He could not have managed without them, and he had come to have a strong devotion to Pamela, well-meaning and loyal as she was. But none of this touched his dreams of the past.

Pamela Colegate often felt insecure and inadequate, and never more so than when she accompanied her husband to Europe. Her triumph was that she remained well-meaning, and never succumbed to jealousy of Anne. What she did experience was a sense of guilt about her – alone, widowed, in England, working hard and going back to her empty flat, while they had their busy family life in Sydney. Whenever Murray bought Pamela any gift, she insisted that he also sent Anne a present of some sort. Anne's long evening coat was the result of Pamela's urging. She had wanted Murray to give his daughter a mink coat.

'My word, Pam, have a heart. Maybe next year. I can't fork out for a mink for Anne just like that in the middle of a trip home.'

'Perhaps not mink then. But she ought to

have a nice fur wrap for evening.'

'If she'd wanted one she'd have bought one. She's comfortably off, don't forget.'

'But she wouldn't spend money on something like that. I told you when you got me my coat–'

'I know you did, dear. And I said one thing at a time, if you don't mind.' He scowled, and disappeared behind the morning paper. But he did not forget, and a day or two later, when he and Anne were having a drink before dinner, he asked her, apparently out of the blue (only she knew him – and Pamela – better), 'Want a fur wra-a-ap for the ball, Anna-Maria?'

'Thanks, Dad, sable will do me fine,' Anne said with a grin. She knew the symptoms. Pamela had been at him.

'Pamela thinks I ought to have got you one,' he remarked guilelessly.

'Pamela's fussing away about her old mink, thinks she filched it off my shoulders, or something.'

'Well, would you like a mink?'

'What would you do if I said yes?' she asked, interested.

'Give my mind to it,' he said, unperturbed. 'Get you one in two-three years, perhaps. If you really wanted it. Don't want to bother unless, though. Could do it, if you liked, so you must say. Trade rates and all that,' he added, to set her mind at ease. 'Patient in the fur trade.'

This was true – or patient's father, to be accurate. A few years earlier the furrier's son would inevitably have died of kidney disease. Colegate had transplanted a kidney from the boy's brother, and both the young men were now leading full and normal lives. The father, incoherent with gratitude, had asked Colegate how he could repay him.

Colegate's demand had been in the nature of a joke. 'Nothing you can do for me, thanks, unless you can lay your hands on a particular sort of artificial kidney. They have one in Seattle, and another in London. That's the lot, so far. We could do with one here. Save more lives that way.'

Nothing daunted, the furrier had put it to his business associates, and forced them to contribute. Within a year, Colegate would have the first maintenance haemodialysis unit in Australia. They hadn't one at the Central, as he irritated them all by pointing out on numerous occasions. 'Yes, they aren't half-bad at routine plumbing down in Fulham,' Ramsay had retorted. One of the objects of Colegate's present trip to London had been to see a similar unit in action in Fulham. 'I agree we don't go in for waste disposal in a big way here,' Ramsay had continued. Colegate remained impervious. 'OK, so I'm a plumber. I'm not ashamed of it,' he had replied. 'After all, what is man? Nothing but a tube, open at both ends.'

The furrier, however, had remained disappointed. He was pleased with his entry into medical finance, but he had wanted to do something for Colegate personally. Eventually, after much pressure, Murray had accepted Pamela's mink, though he had insisted on paying for it. Never had trade rates been so low, though they were prevented from reaching the absolute minimum the grateful father would have liked by Murray's reiterated 'no hanky-panky, now. Trade rates, I said.'

'It's all right, Dad,' Anne reassured him. 'I don't want a mink.'

'What about an evening wra-a-ap though, for this flaming ball?'

'You mean a stole?' Anne giggled. 'I haven't reached that state yet, thanks very much.'

'Why not?' he asked, puzzled.

'Not sufficiently middle-aged – I hope.'

'Pam's only–'

'I know, Dad, but it isn't that.'

'Your mother never had any of the trappings,' he remarked. 'I couldn't have afforded them then. Anyway, she never seemed to need them. But if there is something you'd like – surely there must be some sort of wra-a-ap you'd wear to parties?'

She saw that he was set on giving her something, and told him about the evening coat she hankered after, but had decided she could not afford. Relieved, he had written a cheque there and then, and she had dashed out in the middle of the afternoon and bought it. Murray had been delighted. 'You look as beautiful as your mother,' he had said huskily, his eyes softer than Pamela had ever seen them.

'But Dad,' she protested, trying to keep sentiment at bay (why? she wondered afterwards, and could not tell) 'I'm always supposed to look like you, not mother.'

'Daresay,' he said, 'but you look the way she used to look. I used to forget there was anyone else in the world. She used to have an au-aura.'

Anne said nothing. He paused. 'Who's that fellow Vanstone?' he brought out next. 'What is he? Oh, don't start telling me he's brilliant. Everyone tells me that. What else is he? What sort of a man is he?'

To Anne's relief, since she was not only unwilling but unable to answer these questions, they were interrupted by Pamela, appearing regally in purple taffeta and her vast mink. Shortly afterwards Bill Barham had joined them. He had recently picked up the trick of Anna-Maria from Murray, and said, 'Anna-Maria, you look magnificent. I shall be proud to be seen with you. "Look at Barham," they'll say, "he may not know how to pick nurses, the silly fellow, but he can pick women".'

'Oh, Bill you are mad. But very nice,' she said warmly, and thought how fond of him she was. So that later on the same evening she was thoroughly put out to hear his plan to return to Nyganda. She would be lost if he went away. 'Are you really thinking of going back to Nyganda?' she asked him for the second time, as they danced together shortly after Pamela's gaffe.

'I'm thinking about it seriously,' he admitted. 'It would mean giving up my private practice here, of course. But I like a job I can get my teeth into, and if I'm not going to get the Chair – and there seems no doubt now that I shan't – I wouldn't mind going out there and trying to build up a medical

177

service. Coming with me?'

'Urghh?' She was startled, and sounded it. Bill laughed. He was genuinely amused. 'Too much champagne,' he said. 'You look wonderful, but that is not the dulcet voice in which a beautiful girl accepts – or refuses, for that matter – a proposal of marriage.'

She swallowed. 'Are you proposing to me?'

'That was the general idea. I wasn't suggesting we should both take the trouble to go to Nyganda in order to live in sin. Always been perfectly possible to do that most comfortably here in London,' he added, cocking an experimental eye.

'Oh, Bill,' she said, half touched and half irritated. What did he mean by suddenly proposing to her like this without warning? It had never occurred to her that he wanted to marry her. She had a strong urge to accept him. It would be so comfortable to marry Bill, to have everything settled. And what about Michael? Just root him out of her thoughts? Never again – in a rush, without sorting matters out in her mind, she blurted out, 'Oh, Bill, I can't. I don't see how I can. What about Michael?'

Bill stopped dead in the middle of the floor. He had flown into one of his instantaneous rages, she saw uneasily. The dancers eddied round them, one or two couples brushing close, as they made an unexpected island in the floor.

'Thanks very much indeed,' Bill said gratingly. He raised his hand and for one appalled moment Anne thought he was going to hit her. 'You'd better go and find him, then,' he said, and turned on his heel, leaving her standing.

He was as astounded as she was. He thought he had accepted her feelings for Michael. He had been prepared, as he imagined, to rescue her from him. The unlikelihood of Michael Vanstone bringing her anything but uncertainty and pain, and his own anguished reaction to her misery, had first made him aware of his love for her. Knowing better than she what Vanstone was like, and what he would bring her, Bill had thought himself to be fully armoured. But it was not so at all. He found himself overwhelmed with sheer physical jealousy. He was furious with Anne. Let her get on with it, then. Stupid little idiot. He shouldered his way off the floor, glowering, so that the whispers started. 'Did you *see* Bill Barham?' 'Simply left her *standing*, my dear.' 'Like a thunder-cloud – just *shoved* past. I swear I've got a bruise on my arm.'

He wanted to get away from them all, and pushed his way out to the forecourt, where he stamped angrily round the war memorial and into Russell Square. 'Behaving like a stupid young fool of twenty,' he told himself eventually, reminded of this by the recollection of so many occasions when as a young man he had paced this same square with its great high trees sheltering him, had paced it in fury, distress or anguish – because a girl had rebuffed him, he had run foul of his chief, he had been worried about a patient, had not known where to turn, and once or twice because he had had an unnecessary row with a colleague. 'Go back and make it up,' he had told himself then, and so he told himself now. 'Anne needs you,' he reminded himself. This was not the time for jealousy. He had known her to be in love with Vanstone, it was not news to him, so why had he flown into a rage the moment she admitted it? Simply because he had been childishly offended, he knew. He had wanted her to think only of himself. But Anne was always truthful. And she had been thinking of Michael. He should have expected it. He should not have blurted out his proposal without warning, like some young fool. He should have handled her more cautiously. But he had forgotten all his plans, all his intentions, in her overpowering beauty.

Blast Michael Vanstone. How dared he treat Anne so lightly. How could he grab her love and then deceive her daily with that superficial little doll, Jennifer Ramsay? Only because he was without heart, because for him the Chair of Medicine was a prize in an altogether different category from Anne's love. Let him have the blasted Chair. One day he'd find out what a price he'd paid for it.

Bill's anger with Anne left him as rapidly as it had come. Now he longed only to look after her, to cherish her, to protect her. He went back to the Great Hall to find her. But she had left. Murray had taken her home, Pamela told him. 'She was tired out, poor dear. She looked absolutely white with fatigue. We are going on to breakfast with the Ramsays, but Murray decided to take Anne home first.'

Bill was stricken. All this was his fault.

Here he was mistaken. Anne's shock had come after he had left her. She had gone back to their table, feeling foolish at being left unattended in the middle of the dance floor, but not disturbed. Bill would come round. He always did, from these rages. And the knowledge that he wanted to marry her had left her with a pleasant warm glow, even though she could not tell what she wanted to do about it.

There was no one at their table except Meg. 'Oh, good,' she said when Anne appeared. 'Now you can come too. Look, I was just going to hunt for that wretched Jennifer.'

'Why?'

'Uncle Alec says that after this dance he's going to collect her, and we're all going to the Ramsays' flat for breakfast.'

'What's wrong with that?'

'Only that she's had too much champagne – didn't you notice, last time she was here?'

'Vaguely, I suppose. She was a bit garrulous, I noticed, in a rather silly way, but I didn't pay much attention.'

'Nor did Uncle Alec, fortunately. He had Matron here, and he was talking to her about the training hospital. Then one of the housemen took Jennifer off to dance, and since then she hasn't been back here. Andy says she's in the middle of a group over by the bar, and she's well away.'

'Oh Lord. Silly little fool.'

'We must make someone take her back to

the nurses' home before Uncle Alex gets round to looking for her. We can tell him she's gone to get some sleep before going on duty, and he can push off happily for his little breakfast party. He'd be so horrified if he knew she was drunk, his one ewe lamb. Come on, now, before the dance ends, and they all come back here.'

Glad to be involved in some specific action, Anne followed Meg's coral silk round the Great Hall towards the bar. Sure enough, there was Jennifer, in her pale pink chiffon. 'Suppose she thinks she's cast for the lead in *Sylphides*,' Meg muttered disparagingly.

But it quickly became apparent that Jennifer had cast herself for quite another role, and that she had a fascinated audience encouraging her in it. She was drunk, and her speech was slurred – though obviously perfectly comprehensible to her hearers, and immediately to Meg and Anne.

'Lemme tell you,' she was reiterating, 'you all think me igrant. Doncher? But lemme tell–'

'All right, Jennifer, *we* know,' a tall dark girl said consolingly. 'You've told us. Now come along, there's a good girl.'

'Lemme tell – lizzen. You gotta lizzen.'

'You come along and tell me all about it

on the way,' the dark girl urged. She was the staff nurse on Paterson, Anne thought.

'No, don't spoil it, Sue. It's most entertaining.'

'Yes, leave her alone, Sue. Stop being little-mother-to-all-the-world.'

'Lizzen to me. I'm – I'm grown up.' Jennifer said this with all the solemnity of the drunk, and managed to be surprisingly charming, rather like an erratic four-year-old stumbling and floundering.'

'Of *course* you're grown up, Jennifer darling.'

'But not *quite* used to champagne, perhaps?' someone added nastily.

'Mixing our drinks is what we're not used to,' the girl called Sue said tartly. 'And I blame you for that, Malcolm, you should have had more sense.'

'Don't be so snappish, dear. You're not on the ward now.'

'No, but *really*, Malcolm, you might be some help – suppose her father finds her in this state?'

'Let Vanstone see to it,' Malcolm said with a glint in his eye.'

'Mi'al,' Jennifer said promptly. 'Where's Mi'al?'

'You fool. You've started her off again.'

'Mi'al. Lizzen. You know what?'

'Yes, Jennifer, we *know*. Now come along.'

'No, you don't. Lemme tell you. All think so young, so inesh-eshperience. Eshperienced. Lemme tell, I'm Mi'al's mish-mishtress. Know all about it. Mi'al's mishtress. S'me.'

'Yes, Jennifer, we know. It's marvellous. Now just come along.'

'Gotta stay. Wait for Mi'al. I'm Mi'al's mishtress.'

'No,' Sue said with determination. 'Got to come with me and *look* for Michael.'

This worked.

'Loo' for Mi'al?'

'Yes. This way.'

'This way,' Jennifer said obediently. 'Loo' for Mi'al. I'm Mi'al's...'

'Someone should break it to her,' Malcolm said caustically, 'that the main difference between wives and mistresses is that whereas wives tend to come more or less singly, mistresses can be multiple.' There was a guffaw.

Anne had remained frozen throughout all this. She was vaguely conscious that Meg, originally ahead of her, apparently intending to cross the group and join Sue in her efforts to remove Jennifer, had at some stage turned her back on the lot of them and had been urging her to retreat. But Anne had stood stick still, listening, and had been as resistant to manipulation as Jennifer herself. Now she relinquished her stand and found herself hustled out through one of the long windows into the forecourt. She shivered as the cool night air hit her.

'Our lovely English rose,' Meg said bitterly. 'Well, now you know.'

'Now I know,' Anne repeated automatically.

'I haven't known whether to tell you or not,' Meg said. 'I meant to, the other day. Then I didn't. Anyway, you know now. Better face it, Anne. He's charming, and clever, and one can't help being awfully fond of him. But he's no bloody good to a girl.'

'He's no bloody good,' Anne repeated. As she said it she came to life and her heart cried out in denial. But she kept silent about these cries.

'He's less use than Andy,' Meg continued. She had thought all this out, had been ready to say it for weeks. It was a relief to let Anne know. 'He has nothing to give anyone, and he doesn't even want to take anything worthwhile.'

Two sophisticated, capable young women, expensively and fashionably dressed, they paced sharply round the forecourt of the hospital, both of them torn by love and its failure. Their heels clacked on the paving and the eighteenth century lamps shone on to the blue-green of Anne's dress and the gold of her hair. She felt she was walking on knives. The knives were in her head, too, they had established themselves throughout her body, chopping endlessly, busily, snipping her love into tiny pieces. Snip, snap, that's that. Snip snap.

'He wouldn't even be able to give you as much as Andy's given me,' Meg said again. 'And if he could, I wouldn't recommend it. Don't let's both of us throw our lives away. He's hopeless, I tell you.'

'Hopeless,' Anne repeated. Snip snap.

'He's not worth it,' Meg warned her. 'Simply not worth it. For God's sake don't make a fool of yourself for nothing.'

'For nothing,' Anne said. What was all this about? Nothing. It had all been a mistake. 'A mistake,' she added.

'A mistake,' Meg agreed. 'We all make them. The great thing is not to have to live with them. You're well rid of him,' she asserted. 'Come back to our table now,' she said briskly, 'and we'll find Andy and Bill.' Bill would cope, she thought, he was good at this sort of thing, he'd look after her.

But it was Murray Colegate who took one look at Anne's white face and drove her straight back to her flat. He returned and told Ramsay that she must have been over-working.

'Time she had a holiday,' he said.

'Good idea,' Ramsay said vaguely.

'She won't take one,' Colegate said. 'Says she's too busy.'

'Office *is* busy, of course,' Ramsay agreed. 'But that girl Clare's still there. Difficult for Anne to get away once she's gone to Nyganda. Don't see why she shouldn't go before that, though. Dammit, she's got to be able to take a holiday sometime. She's engaging staff at the moment. Once she's appointed them, no reason I can see why she shouldn't go off and leave Clare to show 'em the ropes.'

'You tell her so, then,' Colegate urged. 'No good me saying anything.'

'All right, Murray, I'll send her packing. Girl has been looking done-up lately, must admit.'

'She worries, you know. About the Nygandans and their problems, and so on.' Colegate had no idea that while Anne took her job seriously and gave considerable thought to it, the Nygandans were perhaps the least of her worries. Like many fathers, he was under the impression he saw straight through his daughter. She was transparent to him. Over-conscientious, she had let the office get on top of her, as women were so apt to do. She needed a holiday. He would take her down to Cornwall.

Chapter 7

In Cornwall the sun shone, yet there was a cool breeze off the sea. The days were long, timeless. The food was wonderful. Anne swam and lay on the rocks in the sun, sauntered back to the little hotel overlooking the estuary for a huge meal, and chatted to Murray and Pamela about nothing in particular.

Sometimes, as she felt physical well-being permeate her like a benison, she thought that this was enough. To be hungry and enjoy the next meal. To have pleasant company. To let the sea support her, and then the sun soak into her. To go to bed at night sleepy with sun and salt air, and to wake in the morning to another day of comfort and pleasure – surely this was enough?

It was not. Yet if it was not, could it be simply her own wilfulness that spoilt it? There was nothing wrong with the life she was leading, only with herself. What was wrong, was that she was hankering after Michael, and yet knew he was not for her. But she had lived for over thirty years without him. Ridiculous to behave as if desolation covered the globe.

To hell with him. She should never have become involved with him in the first place. Just as Meg said, one couldn't help being fond of him, but he was no good. She could see this clearly. She remembered the occasions when she had seen it before. Nothing is going to come of an affair with Michael, she had told herself at least half a dozen times. And nothing had come of it. A pity she had wasted all that effort in hankering after him, waiting there, ready for him to notice or not, as he chose. Ready for him to pick up or put down.

Yet there had been something special between them. Surely they had both shared it? Surely she had not felt this alone? It was impossible. She knew he had shared this.

But then she remembered that while they had apparently shared this affinity, that had been all-important to her, he had been sharing something more fundamental with Jennifer Ramsay. Jennifer must have imagined that her own relationship with Michael had been important, too. Michael had made fools of them both. Or had he made a fool of her alone? Had his affair with Jennifer been serious?

In that case, Anne wondered, why had he taken her out at all? Even in her most nightmarish moments, she knew that he had had some real feeling for her. Even in her deepest depression, she knew that she had not run after him, had not made a nuisance of herself. He could not have felt that he had to escape her. If anything, she had been, in her accustomed fashion, standoffish rather than demanding. Then why? Why, if he had not cared for her, had he taken her about, looked deeply into her eyes, implied that he was hers for life? Why?

Her thoughts went round. Full of impatience, she would rise to her feet, stand poised on the rocks looking out to sea, and then, unable to remain immobile when her thoughts were a prolonged argument in which neither side won, she would go striding along the cliff, trying to shake off the intrusive figure of Michael Vanstone.

Blast Michael. He was no good.

But they had been so happy. Or she had thought they had been so happy. He had surely been happy too – but evidently this happiness had been unimportant to him, had had less meaning than the hot sun now on her salty limbs, or the sight of the sea glittering below the headland covered in gorse.

This could not be true. She could remember so well what he had said to her. No doubt Jennifer could remember equally well what he had said to her.

Had he deceived them both? Had he intended to make fools of them both?

No, of course not, Meg said with certainty. She had come down for the week-end before leaving for her first visit to Ikerobe, though she could hardly spare the time. He had not intended anything like that, she assured Anne. 'He was enjoying himself with you. Jennifer was just because he wanted the Chair of Medicine.'

'But that's much worse. Surely he could get it without that?' Anne jerked the words out furiously. This, if true, was a treachery beyond forgiveness. Spiritual treachery that rendered Michael meaningless to her.

'I expect he could,' Meg agreed. 'But I suppose he thought he would make assurance doubly sure.'

Anne swore, in words it would have shocked Murray Colegate to hear from his daughter. 'What sort of man is he, then? Can he be so calculating?' she ended. 'Never mind me, for once. Think of Jennifer. What about her? What a deceitful way to deal with her. She knows nothing, she's so young. I don't suppose she's ever been in love before. Is he pretending he's in love with her, that she's having a real love affair? He must be. And all the time, you think, he's simply after the Chair of Medicine? Is he going to marry her, pretending it's real, his love, and Jennifer never know anything better? And think he can still carry on with me on the side?' she cried bitterly. Could this worthless materialist be the Michael Vanstone she had known and, once, loved?

'I don't suppose he planned it to that extent,' Meg suggested calmly. 'After all, Jennifer has always thrown herself at his head (from that point of view she's only herself to blame) and I expect he couldn't quite resist playing her along, when she would be so useful to him. That would be exactly like Michael. Andy's always said he's a cold fish. I think that's the crux of it, you know. His feelings aren't warm enough, or strong enough, for any of this to be impossible for him. Jennifer was one pleasant and useful arrangement. You were another, even more pleasant, but of course less useful.'

Anne felt an extraordinary sensation of cold defeat when Meg said this, of negation, of finality. This moment, she afterwards realised, saw the death of her love for Michael.

This was when she abandoned all her attempts to bring back the past, to force life into a love that had gone so hopelessly wrong. For she recognised then, not only with her head but at last with all the longing cells of her body, the truth of Meg's observation. As far as they went, she saw, Michael's feelings had been genuine. This was the explanation of so much that had seemed to her inexplicable. His feelings had been genuine, but not strong enough to bear the weight of the love she had been ready to offer. Not strong enough, in fact, for a lifetime. For him, it had all been pleasant. That was all.

She sighed. 'You're absolutely right,' she agreed sadly. 'I built too much on it. On him.'

'He's very attractive,' Meg said.

Another damning remark. This was all it had been. He was very attractive. She had liked his appearance, and had chosen to read into it all that she hoped to find in life, all that she had been without since Tim's death.

'How juvenile,' she had exclaimed furiously.

And that was the end.

Of course the regret stayed, the sadness

that their summer's happiness was to be sterile, without fruition – like a peach tree in a suburban garden – could only be enjoyed, as Michael had presumably enjoyed it, for itself. It was to have no future. All the hopes she had grafted on to it were dreams never to be fulfilled. This was sad, deeply sad, but peaceful, too. The conflict was over.

She remembered she had felt the same peace once before when she had decided to abandon all thought of a mutual love between herself and Michael, how her life had seemed to become her own again, free of him. She mentioned this to Meg. 'Some part of me, you know, must have sensed that I was forcing the pace,' she commented. 'Part of me must have sensed it was all wrong, otherwise I couldn't have felt like that.'

'I don't think you were forcing the pace,' Meg comforted her. 'I think he was dragging his heels. You were behaving as any normal woman would behave.'

'If you ask me, I was behaving like any silly schoolgirl,' Anne retorted irritably. 'Instead of looking for a real person, who would make a real response, I fixed my eyes on Michael's attractive exterior and saw only what I decided was there. You'd think I'd never known what true love was.' She paused, shocked, as she remembered her life with Tim, and its ending.

Above all, its ending. This she had told no one. She had pushed all knowledge of it away even from herself. This had been a failure too great to be lived with. She had managed never to think about it for years. Now it came back to confront her, in all its original hideousness. She had never come to grips with it before.

She had loved Tim completely, wholeheartedly. She had never thought of any other man. Yet Tim had had an affair with a girl he had met casually. She had discovered this when they were on their last holiday together in the Dolomites. She had accused him, hoping that he would deny it – oh, why hadn't he denied it? But he had not attempted to do this, he had said it was unimportant.

They had fought bitterly. Anne knew she could never forgive him, never trust him again. Part of their love, she cried, had died with his betrayal.

Looking back now to that time six years earlier she could appreciate her underlying rectitude, her self-approval. Only Tim had behaved appallingly.

Their love had been broken off short at that point by death. She was left lost and uncertain, wishing she had forgiven him before they had been separated for ever, yet knowing that no forgiveness could have been sincere.

Given time they would have fought their way through to reconciliation. Looking back now, Anne could tell that some inner core of security, of mutual trust, had remained undisturbed even while she had raged and stormed. But that night, Tim was still very much ashamed of himself. He believed that Anne would probably finish with him, and rightly. He listened to her abuse, and thought it justified. He made no real effort to fight back. He did not know, now, why he had, as she put it, 'betrayed' her. He had known it was a silly thing to do, he knew he would regret it, be ashamed of it. But he had been rather drunk, the girl very seductive and practiced, it had all been so easy, so seemingly inevitable. And, as he tried hopelessly to explain, so unimportant. Meaningless. He could not agree about the betrayal. Anne had lost nothing. Even while he was ashamed, he could not agree that his action held any meaning for her. It had been, and remained, trivial. A brief physical encounter. An explosion, if she liked, of lust. But not a betrayal. It had nothing whatever to do with Anne, or with their love. He should never have done it, he had said he was sorry, he was more than sorry, he was everything she demanded of him. But the act, however regrettable, did not touch her, surely she could see that?

She could not.

Had he lived, his natural resilience, and his certain touch where Anne was concerned, would have brought them together again. He would have bullied her into revealing her inner feelings, which were that however hurt she was she loved him as much as ever. Neither of them honestly felt all was at an end between them. They could not stop loving overnight, and this would have become apparent to both of them. But with the situation unresolved, Tim had been killed.

Anne had known bitter regret. Regret that his affair with this girl had ruined not only their last hours together, but their entire marriage. Regret that even then she had not managed, somehow, to forgive him so that they could have made love during that last night and parted in trust and happiness. Regret that this was what marriage came to, even a good marriage, even her own. Not the slow building of loyalty and faith that she had dreamed, but betrayal, dissolution. She had had no opportunity to make this the beginning of the difficult loyalty that survives, the foundation of a new, no longer untried, love. To her at that time loyalty and faith were not built on failure endured together. In her young surety they were inviolate qualities never to be ruptured.

Perhaps worst of all had been her fear that she had been the cause of his death. Had it been her doing that he had fallen? If he had slept soundly and peacefully that night, would he have returned safely at the day's end? Was it the night spent in accusation and torment, wakeful and unhappy, that had taken the keen edge off his ability when the crisis came? She knew that this must be true. She was responsible.

Then came her own betrayal. She was forced to keep silent about all this, to live a lie – the lie of the perfect love between them, ended by death. She could not shriek to Tim's friends that their love had already ended, that during that last night they lay apart, quarrelling. Nor could she breathe her own recurring horror, her hidden fear of her own inadequacy. Even her loved and trusted Tim had turned to another woman.

Inadequate. She was inadequate. It was this knowledge that had prevented her from remarrying, from trusting another love which might show her this face of herself that she dreaded to see. She was surprised, now that at last she did dare to look at it again, to see this past unhappiness from a different angle. How young she had been – they had both been. Had Tim found her inadequate?

What nonsense. Of course he had not.

Had all these fears been bogeys she had invented and cherished? Had she ruled her life by them? Why had she chosen to love Michael Vanstone? Why Michael of all people? A cold fish, they had warned her. Had she half-known it was true? Had she seen and recognised his own inadequacy, deliberately chosen him because he presented no challenge? Had she seen from the beginning of their most cerebral affair that with him she might safely play at love?

A fine thing then to turn round, heart-brokenly accusatory because she found out that that was exactly what he, too, wanted to do. Was this their mysterious affinity? Did it amount to this alone? Was neither of them capable of anything deeper? Had she ever allowed him to do more than play, or had she been so determined never to step out of her depth that he had had no chance to explore deep waters with her?

He needn't think he has any chance of exploring them with Jennifer, she thought waspishly.

No doubt about it, what she had known with Michael had been a romance, not a love affair. Perhaps Jennifer after all had done better, perhaps they had known reality together? The thought disturbed her. ('I'm Mi'al's mishtress' – did this mean more than the bragging of an inexperienced teenager?) What was Michael really like? She had to face the fact that after all this time she had not the slightest idea.

The person to talk it all over with would be Bill, she thought comfortably, and then stopped suddenly in her tracks. She was to remember for the rest of her life the exact moment she did this. She was sauntering back to the Old Ferry Inn along the path that overlooked the estuary and the sailing dinghies, and she had paused by a clump of wild garlic. Wild garlic, pungent, earthy, unmistakably potent. She began laughing to herself. No more romance, she said sternly. No more building up moments into eternities of subtle meaning. This is wild garlic here by the path, I am going back to the hotel for lunch. That's all there is to it.

At lunch she was more cheerful than she had been for weeks, and Murray Colegate decided that the holiday had done her good. She had been tired out earlier. 'Do you think she works too hard?' he asked Pamela that evening. 'She looked washed out when we arrived, and she doesn't have as much energy as she used to.'

'She's all right, dear. We just caught her at a trying period, when she had a lot on,' Pamela said peaceably. She had more than a shrewd suspicion that Michael Vanstone had been tiring Anne, rather than the office. But if she told Murray this, she knew he would be on the warpath at once.'

'No,' he said dubiously, unconvinced. 'Meg's amazing,' he added. 'Now she always looks as fresh as paint. You can't say nothing disturbs her, because she's obviously upset now, and with reason. I wish she could get free of that chap. He's no good to her. But she always looks blooming.'

'Who looks blooming?' Anne enquired, joining them.

'Meg.'

'Yes, doesn't she? It's amazing. Poor Meg, she's had a terribly tough time, and it doesn't get better.'

'Parents ought to have prevented her from marrying Taussig,' Colegate stated flatly.

'But Dad, how *could* they?'

'Parents can always prevent that sort of thing, if they give their minds to it.'

Anne thought of Meg's parents. Dr Gill was a harassed country G.P., Mrs Gill, when Anne last saw her, faded and ineffectual. She had telephoned Meg from Oxford Street on the day of the housewarming party – of which she had known nothing – saying that she had an hour between trains, and would pop out to Hampstead to see the new house. Meg had been infuriated.

'Of all the times to choose,' she had exploded to Anne, dragging her into the kitchen to relate the circumstances. 'She never comes near me for years, because she disapproves so much of Andy – a lot of help she's been – and then she telephones like this and says she's on her way. I told her I was in the middle of getting ready for the party, and she said "that's all right, darling, I'll only stay a minute, it won't make the slightest difference, you carry on with your preparations, I shan't disturb you". How can she come and not disturb me, at a time like this? And where is she, anyway? Not arrived yet –

lost in the underground, I suppose. She refuses to stay for the party, just to be more difficult, says she has this hour between her beastly trains (she must have used it up by now, I should have thought) and if she could simply have a cup of tea that would be lovely. A cup of *tea,*' Meg had snorted, as though her mother had demanded Napoleon brandy. 'She can have gin and like it.' She paused, recollecting the full annoyance of their conversation. '"I shan't be a nuisance,"' she repeated in tones of loathing. 'She doesn't have to *apologise* for coming. Why can't she behave like anyone else? If she must come today, why can't she fit in and have a drink in a civilised manner, instead of demanding cups of tea and disrupting everything?'

Anne had offered to look after Mrs Gill, and Meg had accepted with obvious relief. 'Oh, if you would,' she had exclaimed. 'I am so afraid of being irritable and horrid to her, and then I shall loathe myself. But you know what it's like, with people arriving and introductions and drinks and people wanting to leave their coats in my room – I simply can't see myself breaking away to do a tour of the linen cupboard and issue cups of char and talk about why I like open-plan and how much I paid for the dining-room table and why I didn't ask her for the old gate-legged table in the garage.'

Anne sniggered. 'Is it still there.'

'Heavens yes, and full of worm. But waiting for *me*. She thinks modern furniture is vulgar – only she won't actually say so, of course, only look down her nose sadly – not to mention extravagant, and she simply won't understand the set-up at all.'

She didn't. Anne caught sight of her, her bun drooping under her squashed felt, with her faint air of lost and ravaged beauty, peering about the room vaguely. She kissed Anne thankfully and affectionately. 'Thank goodness *you're* here – how nice you look, darling.' Mrs Gill herself was wearing an excellent old suit from Burberry's she had possessed for twenty years, with a faded dog's tooth pattern, and her baum marten ties, that she had always worn when she had come to visit them at school. She was hung round with nylon bags full of parcels from Selfridge's Food Store, Marks and Spencer, and Debenham's, and accompanied by an overpowering smell of coffee – she had also found time to go to Yarner's. 'I'm afraid I'm not very welcome in the middle of all this,' she regretted, gesturing agitatedly, 'but I simply had to see the house. I must say, this *is* a change, isn't it?'

'I promised Meg I'd show you round,' Anne said. 'In case she couldn't get away for long enough. Would you like a drink first, or–?'

'No, no drink, than you, Anne. You know what my head is like. And I've so little time before my train. Just show me the house, that's all I've come for. Then I can tell Harold about it.' Mrs Gill had obviously been terrified of the blast of sound that had greeted her, and the chink of glasses. 'I did so want to see the house,' she murmured, abashed now, 'but I'm afraid this is *quite* the wrong time to have chosen. Meg did say – but I didn't quite realise – and it seemed such an opportunity, before the fares go up again, you know, to do some shopping and see the house. Only I'm afraid I should have rung up earlier. But it's so much cheaper to telephone once I've reached London, you see, I didn't think. Especially now Meg isn't working any more, and it isn't a question of her day off. And then telephoning was so very complicated. Oh dear, I don't like these new telephones at all. Such peculiar noises. I *was* relieved to hear Meg's voice. I never thought I should get through at all. It was all so *difficult*.'

Remembering all this, Anne had repeated, 'Honestly, Dad, I don't see how on earth the Gills could have stopped Meg marrying Andy. Nothing would have stopped them, least of all Meg's parents. They were absolutely determined, although we all knew it was bound to turn out badly. There was nothing any of us could do.'

'I'd have done something,' Colegate said calmly.

'You're like Bill,' Anne said. 'He thinks he's going to stop Clare and Onajianya marrying. But I doubt if he will, in the long run.'

'At least he's trying,' Pamela said. She had met Clare, and deeply disapproved of her proposed marriage. 'Her parents ought to *forbid* it,' she asserted.

'But *look–*' Anne began.

'If any daughter of *mine–*' Colegate said at the same moment. They stopped and glared at one another.

'*Honestly,* Dad, if I wanted to marry Onajianya, you wouldn't *stop* me, would you?' Anne demanded. 'What possible excuse–'

'Don't need to have an excuse. Nothing to do with Onajianya as an individual. No daughter of mine is going to marry an African. Or go to live in Africa, for that matter.

I wouldn't let Meg go, if I were Taussig, for instance. No place for a woman – European woman. Madness.'

'But Dad – you sound like some old Colonel Blimp, chuntering away in some Edwardian club-room, wah wah wah.' She stared at him. The gap between the generations had never seemed so impassable.

'My dear girl, it's sheer common sense. Nothing to do with prejudice.'

'Not *much*,' Anne muttered.

'Any man would be depressed at the prospect of his daughter marrying someone who proposes to take her to live in Africa. Look at the Congo. How could you ignore the danger? I'd have fits if you said you were going to marry a missionary out there, let alone an African. I'd be callous if I didn't worry.'

'It might be safer to marry an African than a missionary,' Pamela pointed out realistically.

'It might, or it might not. We don't know. We don't know what's going to happen.'

'But you wouldn't suggest keeping all your children perpetually wrapped in cotton wool,' Anne exclaimed irritably. 'If it was your son we were talking about, you'd feel quite differently. No father would try to keep a son at home if he wanted to go to Africa. What's more, though there might be an immense amount of gossip, no one would really mind if he married an African wife–'

'I should.'

'No, you wouldn't, not really. Not if she was a pleasant girl, educated and attractive. It's this antediluvian attitude to *daughters* that infuriates me. Lock up your daughters.'

'Not a bad idea at all,' Murray murmured.

'Meg, Clare and me – we're free, white and twenty-one. Why can't we lead adventurous lives and break new ground, just as much as the men?'

'Votes for women,' Pamela commented dryly. 'Count me out, anyway, dear. Coming to England is adventure enough for me. But I agree with Murray, I'm afraid, I'd feel very uneasy if I was this girl Clare's mother. I wouldn't half talk to her for her own good. But I expect,' she ended, 'that would only have the effect of making her keener still to go, and go she would.'

'If she were worth anything at all, she would. That's what you don't seem to realise, Dad. I was talking to Bill about it, and he agreed that all one could do was to let Clare experience Nyganda at first hand, to give her a chance of distinguishing between her love for Onajianya and the lure of strange continents and strange cultures.'

'Lure,' Murray repeated, in a disparaging drawl. 'Women are the maddest creatures.'

'Not at all, dear, I see exactly what Anne means, and men are much sillier in that particular way,' Pamela said crisply, thinking of Murray's own English marriage, and the lure that England still held for him.

'You know,' Anne went on, 'I think some girls feel something much more important than the glamour of strange countries. Somewhere inside them they know that an ordinary marriage to someone from their own background is simply not enough, is never going to satisfy them. They're looking for strange demanding marriages as much as they look for strange demanding careers. All their friends cluck agitatedly and say they are throwing themselves away. What they mean is they could have married a successful stockbroker or an up and coming consultant, certain to make money and give them prosperity. They could be hostess to nice dinner parties of well-heeled guests in Surrey, raise children to be educated at the public schools, play golf, go on ski-ing holidays and cruises, run several cars and an *au pair* girl. *Ugh.* Just because girls are pretty and superficially conventional, like Meg or Clare, people assume they are absolutely cut out for a pretty, safe, conventional life. But their looks are totally misleading. They know they can easily get that sort of life, and they don't want it. They know it would be a dead bore. They'd feel suffocated in it. And it would be bad for them, bring out the worst in them. They'd turn into dissatisfied drifters, always looking for what they'd never had, complaining about nothing and irritating their children. Look at Meg. She's unhappy now. But her regrets come from having lived, from having explored for herself, not from suburban emptiness. She's *alive*.'

'And long may she remain so,' Colegate said gently. 'That's my small point. Pretty basic, it seems to me.'

'You've got something there, dear,' Pamela had agreed. Anne gave up the attempt to make either of them understand her point of view. But she had not finished with the subject, and as soon as she was back in London she reopened it with Bill. She buttonholed him urgently the minute she saw him, pausing in the hall after a ward round.

'I was thinking, Bill,' she said. 'You know how worried we've all been about Meg. But

I was saying to Dad – only he couldn't see what I meant at all – at least Meg's *alive*.' She remembered her father's caustic remark. 'Full of life, I mean,' she amended hastily. 'Bursting with it. She's never stagnated. It suddenly seemed to me that that's what matters most to her. We're quite wrong to pity her. She's got what she wanted. We all say poor Meg, what a time she's had with Andy, what a dreadful mistake to have married him, what a much better life she could have had, and so on. But all the time she's alive, things are happening to her, she's changing, she's experiencing life at first hand.' She looked at him suspiciously, suddenly becoming aware of her own enthusiasm and wondering if she sounded like some earnest lecturer on careers to fifth forms – which would never do for Bill.

But he showed no sign of the tolerant amusement she half-expected. 'One thing you can say about those two, I agree with you,' he answered at once. 'They may be unhappy, but they live life to the full. And after all, it's normal, you know, to be unhappy as well as happy. Life is full of sadness. Only harm ourselves if we turn our backs on it and push it away with central heating and cocktail parties. Life's full of disillusion, of people who fail to get their heart's desire and have to come to terms with reality.'

'I wouldn't exactly say they've come to terms with anything, or anyone. Certainly not each other.'

'No, but they're on the way to it. They have a living painful relationship, apparently unbreakable. One day they'll get it worked out.'

'Unbreakable? They've just broken it.'

'You wait and see.'

'Do you think they'll come together again, then?'

'Wait and see.'

'I wouldn't know whether to be glad or sorry if they did,' Anne began.

'Doesn't matter which you are,' he interrupted. 'They'll be living it, not you. You try living your own life. Andy and Meg are quite capable of working out their own future. What about you, what are you going to do?'

'Me?' she heard herself repeat in a foolish bleat.

'Yes, you, Anna-Maria Heseltine. What are you going to do with the next bit of your life?'

'Next bit—'

'Are you going to sit around waiting for

that brilliant and successful young fraud to get the Chair of Medicine, and hope you can be Lady Vanstone eventually (if someone with less beauty but more initiative and drive doesn't beat you to it, and if that pedant ever gets around to marrying at all)–'

'Really, Bill, you're being impossible. And most unfair. You've no right–'

'Perfect right to speak my mind. Are you going to settle down to dreary eminence, or are you coming out to Nyganda with me, and we'll throw worldly success back to the pontiffs in that nasty new building in Regent's Park? Of course, you'd be joining the ranks of the unhonoured and unsung – no K's for the field workers.'

'Bill, what are you talking about?'

'My dear girl, surely it's plain enough? And it isn't as if I haven't asked you before, either. I'm trying to persuade you to marry me and come out to Nyganda.'

'But are you really going to Nyganda?'

'To hell with whether I'm going to Nyganda or not – yes, I am, in fact. Will you give me an answer to my perfectly clear proposal, instead of ignoring it? For God's sake, do I have to go on repeating it time after time?'

Under all the bombast, she suddenly saw, he was frightened. Frightened that she was going to refuse. A wave of affection swept over her and she felt she could not bear to hurt him.

'Yes please,' she said, and gave him a brilliant smile.

'Thank God. Are you sure that's all right? You don't really want to marry the future professor, do you?' Unexpectedly, his eyes became hard, keen and watchful, they stared intently through her.

'No,' she said. 'I don't.'

'Do much better with me, you know,' he remarked. 'And that's the truth, prejudiced though I may be.'

'I know,' she agreed. She did know. This, after all, was what she had worked out in Cornwall. The Michael Vanstone she had thought she knew was nothing but her own romantic delusion. Bill was reality. He was the future, a future of hard work, shared effort – and shared fun. For there would be a lot of fun with Bill, there always had been. Warmth, too, and steady affection.

Apparently Bill could read her like a book. 'You'll get used to the idea,' he now re-marked, with a gleam in his eye. 'You may even grow to like it.'

'Of course I like it,' she retorted indignantly.

'You looked as you might have looked at the age of ten or so, preparing to take a header off the high diving board. Panicked, but at the same time resolute.'

'Well, I am panicked but resolute. I don't imagine it'll be any soft option to be married to you.'

'That's my girl. It won't be. You'll hate me often, I expect.' He appeared quite satisfied with the prospect. 'I'm a very annoying man,' he added, in the tones of one imparting a not unpleasing discovery.

'I know, thank you.'

'I know you do. As for you, you're a buttoned-up, stiff-upper-lip, over-correct introvert.'

'Oh,' she said dully.

'Not to worry. I shall soon be able to correct all that, and you'll feel much more comfortable as a result.'

She looked startled. 'I expect you're absolutely right,' she admitted. 'Er – may one ask how you propose to set about changing it?'

He made a brief succinct reply, and added, 'plenty of that works wonders always.'

'I don't really think,' Anne suggested, 'that we can continue this conversation here in

217

the hall. I find it a little inhibiting.'

'I don't,' he replied boomingly.

'No, I can see you don't. But I *do*, Bill, and if you don't mind I'd rather we went elsewhere to work out all these fascinating possibilities for our future.'

'So far I've only mentioned one. Glad to know you find it fascinating, though. Don't try to shush me. I warn you here and now it's useless. No point in you wasting time on that for the rest of your life. I say what I like, and if people don't like it, they know what they can do.'

'–off, no doubt,' Anne said quietly, her lips quirking.

'That's it, my girl. Glad you're getting the idea. Always said you were quick in the uptake.'

'Please can we go somewhere *else* and have some lunch?'

'Lunch? Lunch? Of course. Why didn't you say so before? Come along. Celebration lunch. Splendid idea. Where the hell's m'car got to?'

The porter, who had been hovering and who Anne was convinced had heard every word of their conversation, now managed to materialise under Bill's nose, and said, 'You came on foot this morning, sir.'

'What? What?'

'Came on foot this morning, sir.'

'Good God, so I did.'

'Shall I call you a taxi, sir?'

'Good idea, good idea, yes, by all means.'

'Anyone would think you were setting up as the absent-minded professor,' Anne remarked, when they were settled in a taxi making its way by fits and starts down a crowded Kingsway.

'No Chair of Medicine for Barham,' he said promptly. 'Barham has boobed. Down with Barham.'

'Oh, Bill, it's not as bad as that. Listen, what *is* all this about Nyganda? You really must tell me.'

'Just that I'm thinking of going back there.'

'Permanently, do you mean?'

'More or less. For years, anyway. Thing is, got to face it, I'm not going to get the Chair, this stupid trouble over the students has put paid to that. Of course, I might not have stood a chance anyway, probably Vanstone has been a dead certainty all along. But if I did have a chance, I haven't any longer. It only needed some little thing to weight it against me, and the lousy in intake of nurses I sent over this year has done that all right.'

'Oh Bill, why did you have to let it happen?' Anne wailed.

He gave her an odd look. 'I don't have any instinct about that sort of thing, you know.'

'But you must have. I don't believe it. Surely you guessed there was something fishy going on?'

'No, I didn't notice at all. I was busy, and a good deal of the time I was away. There's always a lot of fiddling going on, anyway, of one sort of another. It never occurred to me that this was a bigger fiddle than usual.'

'The trouble with you, you know, Bill, is that you don't have enough principle.' Anne suddenly realised that she had always known this about him, though she had never put it into words before. 'You – they all say it at the Central – you're the great extemporiser, the one who sweeps up other people's muddles and somehow out of a chaotic shambles produces some sort of working model. Very imperfect, but adequate. And *working*. It's a wonderful gift, but you're so busy knocking up these rough and ready solutions that you're apt to be unscrupulous. So sometimes you land yourself in a mess – and other people too – simply because you're so used to making the best of a bad job that you don't always notice how appallingly bad a job you're dealing with this time – so bad that no one else would touch it with a barge pole. You just have a bash, in your usual style.'

'Quite right. I don't expect things to be perfect. Or even anything approaching perfect. I'm much more interested in making them work than in seeing that everything is shipshape and above-board, and that there's nothing anyone could take exception to, or advantage of. I don't honestly care if they do take advantage, or if they don't like what I'm doing. What I want is action. If we can't move forward, let's try moving back or sideways. Crabwise, if necessary. Anything is better than inertia.'

They had reached Maiden Lane, and he paid off the taxi and steered her into Rule's, where somehow he managed to make them find him a table. Anne heard murmured colloquies. 'No time to telephone – patients – special celebration – in confidence, must tell you ... nowhere else possible, of course...' mutter mutter, and his wallet came suggestively out of his pocket.

Finally they were seated and Bill had ordered.

'More bribery and corruption,' Anne remarked with a grin.

'Not at all. They found us a table because they *liked* me, he said, his face taking on an air of sottish benevolence.

'Oh, yeah? Anyway, to go back to the Nyganda situation, I must say, you'll have to be more careful, Bill. One of these days–'

'Something really awful will happen,' he said heavily, making his mouth round and his eyes pop out.

'It's not just a joke,' she said crossly.

'My darling girl, what do you suppose I'm marrying you for?'

'Eh?'

'To see to all that sort of thing, of course. No one could be more scrupulous than you. Right?'

'I – I don't know. Me?'

'Well, I'm telling you. You are. So you'll see to all that side of things and keep a tight rein on me and my activities. That's what I need you for.'

'I see.' And she did. He was right. Bill could jolly anyone along, but in the background he needed guidance and a restraining influence. He needed someone rigid and with unfaltering standards. Herself.

'How horribly priggish I must be,' she said reflectively.

'Oh no, you aren't. You just have a streak

222

of unalterable integrity running right through you. I respect it. No joking. I do. And need it. Hope you've enough for two.'

She felt better. Bill could always reassure one, she thought warmly, and smiled at him with all her heart. To her amazement, his face grew hard, taut, controlled. She stared.

'Look at me like that,' he stated, 'no alternative but to take you straight home to bed.' He paused, and she felt desire spring across the table between them. 'You've never looked at me like that before, do you know? What I've been waiting for,' he added, and suddenly she saw he was alight with triumph. 'I'll show you,' he said.

The waiter arrived with the cheese board.

'Ah,' he said, switching his attention instantly. 'Now let's see … um…'

When the waiter had departed, they had their cheese and Bill had refilled her glass, Anne ventured another try at the question of his return to Nyganda.

'Nyganda?' he queried. 'Um, yes, well – told you, didn't I?'

'You said you might go back for some years,' she prompted.

'Yes. Well, that's it. It's not how I had expected my career to end. If anyone had told me five years ago that that's what I'd come to, I'd have been horrified. Fact. Failure, I'd have thought it. But I'm all washed up here. I don't want to sit around watching the young men pass me, seeing Vanstone make the Professorial Unit a sterile outfit of damned statisticians and bio-chemists, listen to him telling the students to be careful and cautious and above all keep their fingers clean. They tell me he calls me a confidence trickster.'

Anne was startled. She knew the nickname, of course, but it had never occurred to her that Bill was aware of Michael's unkind reference to him.

'Let me tell you,' he banged the table, 'I'd rather be a confidence trickster and keep the patients happy than spread deadly alarm on my ward rounds, leaving behind me a collection of frightened human beings convinced their next stop is the morgue, simply because I'm so bloody locked on to watching my own unspotted lily-white reputation that I daren't utter a few cheery words in case they might mislead some poor beggar who's going to die one day. All Vanstone's patients die a thousand deaths, you know that?'

Anne mumbled.

'And young Wooldridge has to go round

after him and try to convince them that they've got a few more days on earth. I ask you, what kind of doctoring is that?'

'He's over-scrupulous,' Anne said. 'Just as you're not scrupulous enough.'

'I'd rather be me,' he said simply.

Anne looked at him and decided he was right.

'You can't expect to be able to help people and not get your hands dirty occasionally,' he pointed out.

She wondered how much of a price Bill himself paid for his continual immersion and interference in the lives of all around him – that everyone asserted came so easily to him. Probably, she decided, he paid less of a price than Michael paid for doing nothing. She couldn't help feeling that in this event the practical move appeared to be to act.

'I've spent a year – or nearly a year – in Nyganda,' Bill was saying, 'and it's changed my outlook. The need there is fantastic. It's crying out to be met – somehow, by anyone. You can't go wrong. All you need is a pair of hands. Do you know, for instance, that except when one of our chaps goes out there on tour, there's not a single radiologist in the country? That's for a population of ten million? Nor an anaesthetist, nor a bacteriologist? Every physician and surgeon out there has to be able to turn his hand to anything. After all – just as you said – I am the great improviser. I'm just the lad for Nyganda. All I have to do is to farm out my private practice, and I can be off. If you agree, that is?'

She was ready to give him her formal and considered blessing, but he paused only momentarily. 'You do, of course,' he stated emphatically, on her behalf.

She smiled. How like him this was, he threw himself and anyone near him wholeheartedly into anything he did. How confident he was, how little of the sceptic.

'After all, you're specially trained for Nyganda,' he was saying. 'Extraordinarily farsighted of me to put you in that job. Couldn't be better. It's useful you're such a healthy wench, too. Easily able to stand the life.'

'Oh,' Anne said in a small voice, 'shall I?'

'Easily,' he said expansively.

'You don't – um – see me as fragile, at all?'

He roared with laughter. 'Strong as a horse,' he asserted.

'Aren't you going to look after me?' Anne asked. 'You know, protect me, see to my comfort?'

'Got it all wrong, old dear. That's what you're going to do for me.'

'Oh.'

'I want that clear from the beginning,' he said, and roared again.

'All right,' she said, grinning in spite of herself. 'You've made it clear. I get the message. Now you make something clear to me. When is all this going to happen?'

'All what?' he asked, bewildered.

'Us marrying, and going to Nyganda, and me doing all this looking after you?'

His eyes gleamed. 'First, us marrying – day after tomorrow. I'll get a special licence. Going to Nyganda – about a year from now, I'd say. It'll take me a year to pull out, what with the medical school and the practice.'

'So there's no real hurry about anything,' Anne said thoughtfully.

'Plenty of hurry about getting married,' he said. 'No point in hanging about. The sooner I get you–'

'Bill. Stop it. Now please be sensible.'

'Don't intend to be sensible. No need.'

'Listen, Bill. I have to tell Dad, and Pamela.'

'They'll let you telephone from here,' he said affably. A thought struck him. 'When does Murray go back down under?' he asked.

'Next month.'

'There you are then. We must get married while he's still here, and we must fit in a honeymoon before term begins. Where'd you like to go?'

'I don't know if I *can*,' she protested. 'I've just had a fortnight's holiday, and Clare's left for Nyganda. The new staff know *nothing*.'

'Try to cultivate a sense of proportion,' he said placidly. 'You are coming with me on our honeymoon. They'll have to manage without you. Damn lucky to be getting you back afterwards. Take a month's leave without pay. We can get married the first week in September. Anything wrong with that?'

'No.' She was surprised how easy it seemed to be when Bill took over. The future was suddenly assured and pleasing. Full of change, but she could meet it with confidence. It was years since she had felt like this. She realised she should make an effort to share her mood with him. 'It's years since I've felt like this,' she announced shyly.

'Like what?'

'Looking forward to everything like this.'

'My darling love,' he leant forward across the table, as though he would crush it into the floor and take her into his arms. For a moment she almost expected this to happen. 'I should have married you years ago.'

'Now will do,' she said demurely.

'Yes, well, we'll both go and see Murray,' he decided, and beckoned the waiter for the bill.

But Murray and Pamela, they found, had already left Charles Street for Haslemere. They were spending the week-end with the Ramsays at Densworth. Bill was quite happy to pursue them, but Anne stalled. She thought Jennifer would be there, and she didn't want to meet her at present. So they decided to keep their news to themselves over the week-end, tell the Colegates on Monday and after that put an announcement in *The Times*. 'And that'll be the end of our privacy,' Bill pointed out. 'After that it'll be one long round of dinners and horrid little parties, so we might as well enjoy our spot of peace before the storm.

'So that's how you look on our approaching marriage?'

They were walking along Charles Street. He stopped abruptly, clasped her firmly to him and began kissing her. After a brief protest she began to enjoy herself so much that she forgot the spectacle they presented.

'There,' he said finally, releasing her but holding her still by the elbows to steady her – a necessary precaution. 'How long I've wanted to do that. What a satisfactory armful you are. Let's go back to your flat now.' He hailed a taxi and bundled her into it.

Chapter 8

At Densworth that week-end Isobel Ramsay and Pamela Colegate got on tolerably well. They pottered argumentatively about the house and garden while the two men lost themselves in prolonged discussions about medicine.

The talk was interspersed with the sort of meals they had at Densworth. Isobel Ramsay always provided plenty of food at frequent intervals. She never stinted on quantity. But the quality was another matter. The Ramsays lived on the type of diet supplied at a small boys' prep school.

'Stodge, that's what it is, stodge,' Colegate complained to Pamela when they were dressing for dinner on the second evening. 'Here I am, dressing up in a bloody dinner-jacket as if we were going some place, and all we'll do is eat food that's worse than what they used to give us in the army, and drink the cheapest wine the Victoria Wine Stores can rustle up, sandwiched between glass after glass of excellent whisky. Never mix grain and grape, I was always told, but Ramsay doesn't care.'

'They're the nicest people,' Pamela said, 'but you can't get away from it, their food is lousy.'

'Atrocious,' Colegate substituted.

'I suppose this is what people mean when they complain about English cooking,' Pamela mused. 'It'll be an experience to tell them all back home, anyway. Now I know why it's an international joke. It isn't as if the Ramsays couldn't afford decent food, either – or drink.'

'It doesn't occur to Isobel,' Colegate pointed out. 'And Alec's got other things to think about.' They went down to dinner. It was a cool August evening, and both women wore their mink stoles and extended their strapping legs to the one-bar electric fire that sat forlornly in the great pseudo-Tudor inglenook fireplace. Ramsay poured generous glasses of whisky, and Pamela shivered and took a gulp, saying immediately, 'Well, at least that warms my gullet. This climate of yours gives me the creeps.'

Isobel Ramsay was unmoved, and neither sent for an additional fire nor closed the open window on the far side of the room. 'Food will soon warm you up,' she asserted.

They went in to dinner. No nonsense about soup or *hors d'oeuvres*, ever, at Densworth. They plunged straight into the main course, which tonight turned out to be cottage pie, with additional boiled potatoes, cabbage, and a very small dish of beans from the garden. This was washed down by Spanish burgundy, and followed by baked jam roll. After this they went back to the drawing-room and the electric fire and drank small cups of tepid and watery Nescafé poured from an imposing silver pot. Uncle Alec returned to the whisky decanter, while Isobel broke a bar of Cadbury's milk chocolate and handed it round.

Pamela Colegate surveyed the two men in dinner-jackets and her hostess, in a no longer new brocade suit, with her stole clapped firmly on her shoulders, and thought: the English at home. At last I've seen it. What a tale for the girls.

'Shall we have a game of Scrabble?' Isobel now asked, munching the last square of chocolate.

Uncle Alec at once took evasive action and removed himself, Colegate and the whisky decanter to his study. 'Isobel will not learn,' he complained. 'I won't play that game. I've told her again and again, and she's usually excellent over that sort of thing. But this is one habit I've never been able to break. Whenever we have visitors in the house, she suggests that damned game after dinner. Can't think why. Ever played it? No? Lucky fellow. Stupid waste of time. I've never had so much time on my hands that I've wanted to pass it in silly pointless futile games of Scrabble. Daresay I may get round to it after I've retired. Doubt it, though. Hoping to follow up a good many loose ends I've not had time for yet. Got notebooks full of them. Can't tell you how much I'm looking forward to it. Not to be under pressure any longer. This contemporary rush and tear doesn't suit me. I don't like it, you know. Hardly ever have a chance to take things easy and see m'friends. Looking forward to doing that when I retire, too. Catch up on a lot of old friends I don't manage to meet more than once every few years. Like you.' He began to enumerate others, and they worked their way through men they had both known to the younger generation. Murray Colegate saw the opportunity he had been waiting for.

'What can you tell me about this chap Vanstone?' he asked. 'I meet him all over the place, and they all tell me he's brilliant. Can't quite make him out, myself. A bit too much the conventional Englishman for me. Perhaps I'm doing him an injustice. But he looks like being my son-in-law, and I can't say I'm altogether happy about it.'

Uncle Alec began lighting his pipe. When he had completed the operation with some care, he blew several smoke rings, watching them sail up one after the other, rounded and perfect. Then he said gently, 'You interest me considerably, Murray. You know, I was under the impression that Vanstone was shortly going to be *my* son-in-law, and I must confess I was fairly happy about it.'

'Wha-a-at?' Colegate uttered a long exclamation. 'The bastard. If I get hold of him – my God, Alec, I'm sorry if I've opened my mouth at the wrong – no, dammit, I'm not sorry. It looks as if it's about time we got together over Vanstone. If he's been chasing after both our daughters at the same time, the sooner we know it the better for them. And the worse for him.'

'He's known Jennifer since she was quite a small child, of course,' Ramsay said slowly. 'He's been going around with her lately, and certainly she's been taking it seriously.' He sighed. 'Whether she should have done, I don't know. Must admit, though, I thought m'self that he wouldn't take her out unless

he intended to settle down with her. Not –
um – suitable. Thought he'd have some
respect for me, y'know. Old-fashioned of
me, perhaps. Jenny cares for him, I know
that. Thinks she's going to marry him. Told
Isobel so.'

'Anne cares for him, as far as Pamela and I
can tell. That's why I wanted your opinion.'

'Did you discover if he and Anne intended
marriage?' Ramsay asked heavily.

'No. She won't confide in me. But Pamela
and I both thought it was fairly serious, and
I asked Meg Taussig about it – she's usually
in Anne's confidence, you know. She said
they were in love.'

'Must put our heads together,' the old man
said firmly. 'Glad you mentioned it. Good
thing to know where you stand. First of all,
ought to be fair to Vanstone. Young man can
take out two young women without promising either of them a thing, eh? Trouble is,
he's not such a young man, and Jenny's still
a very young girl. May be prejudiced, after
all, I am her father and that makes a considerable difference to one's attitude, but
I've never cared for a sophisticated middle-
aged chap making a fool of a young girl,
h'm?'

'Never thought I'd live to hear meself say

it, but it's *not done*,' Murray agreed, with a sharp sarcastic smile.

'Nonsense to say he couldn't help it, of course he could. Must say I find the situation very unexpected. Always thought of him as completely reliable where Jenny's concerned. Knew nothing of him taking out Anne. Can't think how I haven't heard.'

'I'm sorry if I've raised a complication,' Murray said heavily. 'No one said a word to me about Vanstone and Jennifer. It never crossed my mind she was involved, or of course I'd never have brought the matter up. Come to think of it, you know, people have seemed a bit embarrassed when I started asking about Vanstone. I noticed it all right, but I put it down to the fact that here was this blundering Aussie muddling in where no Englishman would tread, asking questions about the impeccable Vanstone – you know, old school tie stuff. Perhaps it wasn't that at all.'

'We must ask someone. Get it out of them. It's probably a situation that everyone except Isobel and myself – and I hope poor Jenny too – has been discussing for months. You know what the Central is.' He paused, and added, 'One thing's certain, I'm not going to have Jenny hurt. She's very young, and she's been sheltered. Too sheltered, perhaps. She's a nice child, you know, Murray, but very ignorant still. Well-meaning, and a trier. A bit like Isobel, though – sometimes she hasn't a clue, poor scrap. I thought Vanstone'd look after her.'

'Probably he will,' Murray said comfortingly. 'It may simply be that he hasn't got round to taking her seriously yet. She is so young.' He, too, was trying to be fair, in meeting this unexpected complication that he had not at all foreseen. 'I'd be relieved if there was no question of Anne settling down with Vanstone. He's not the right man for her, in my opinion. Afraid I may have raised a bit of a storm in a teacup – all the same, Meg did tell me–' he broke off, frowning.

'What did Meg tell you?' Ramsay demanded.

'She said she hoped it wouldn't come to marriage. That's really what started me on my investigation. She said–' he broke off again, as he remembered Meg's voice urging 'he's no good to her, she's fallen for him and she's blind. He's clever and he's charming, and women do like him, but he'll just make a fool of Anne.'

'What did she say?' Ramsay asked implacably.

'She said he'd make a fool of Anne,' Murray repeated grudgingly, all his dislike of Michael Vanstone coming to the surface again.

'I must look into this,' Ramsay said with decision. 'If Meg thinks that, there must be a good deal about Vanstone that I don't know. Of course, you do get that, don't you find yourself? By the time you're as senior as we are, all the young men present their best side to you. Sometimes you get a shock when you get a sidelight on them from one of their contemporaries, however well you think you know them. They're different people. I'll ask Andy Taussig about this. He'll know. I thought I understood Vanstone. Come to think of it, though, I know nothing about his behaviour with women. Certainly he's always been spoken of as a charmer. They used to tease him about it when he was younger. Perhaps that should have warned me.'

'I may have misled you,' Murray said scrupulously, hard though it was for him to say this, and angry as the thought made him. 'He may know exactly where he is with Jennifer, and be wanting to marry her.' (After all, he thought, most men would not fool around with their chief's daughter. Just let any of his young men think they could try it on, for instance. If only he had his damned daughter out in Sydney with him, there'd be none of this nonsense.) 'He may have been having a flirtation with Anne – who I'm afraid has taken it seriously – but be fully intending to marry Jennifer.' He was hating Vanstone as he spoke, and unknown to him his voice vibrated with this unuttered venom.

'Oh yes, he may,' Ramsay agreed. 'But it's not good enough, is it? Anne's a fine girl. I'm very fond of her, and she's worth far more than a flirtation with Vanstone while he fills in time waiting for Jenny to grow up. Damn it. I won't have it. What an outlook for my poor Jenny. What sort of marriage would she have with him, if he's got into the habit of this sort of thing?'

Murray sighed, and said, 'Meg didn't give me any details – damn these girls, why can't they tell you the whole story? – but I wonder now if she meant that Anne wasn't quite certain in her own mind about Vanstone? And a good thing, too, as it turns out.'

'I'm afraid,' Ramsay said slowly, 'Jenny is only too certain about him.' He knocked out his pipe and blew through it. 'I won't have him muddling her about,' he said with finality. 'On Monday I shall make it my business to find out what's been going on, and if it's what we think it is, I shall have a straight talk with young Michael. After that he can go away and think things over. And he needn't come back unless he's prepared to deal fairly with Jenny, however upset she is about it in the meantime.'

'Will he carry out what you tell him?'

'He'd better,' Ramsay said succinctly. 'In any case, he will,' he added in more friendly tones. 'I've not been completely mistaken about him, you know. I wouldn't be surprised–' he was getting over his shock and beginning to see the picture and the people involved clearly '–if some of this isn't Jenny's own doing.' He chuckled. 'She's always admired him, and I daresay she's been chasing him. I did think that, once or twice, I remember. She's an attractive young minx, these days, and he may have been flattered, enjoyed being looked up to, eh? Now your Anne – even if she loved him, she wouldn't look at him with awe, d'you think? Jenny does. Daresay the silly young fool thought he could manage the two of them, and then suddenly found it all too much for him eh?' He began laughing, and Murray found himself reluctantly laughing with him. In fact, Ramsay had ceased to be disturbed. Jenny was young, he would see that she was all right, and as for Michael – well, fortunately there was no harm done. He'd have a talk with the young devil, and lay down the law a bit. Good thing he and Murray had had their little chat. 'If there's been anything wrong with Michael Vanstone,' he remarked, musing now on one of his young men, as he often did, 'it's that he's become over-confident. He's had it too easy. He's sailed through life, passing his exams well, getting his house jobs at the Central, getting his membership first try, now his fellowship, always the blue-eyed boy on the up and up. Might do him good to have a set-back. Humanise him. By George, you know what I'll do? I'll separate them. Young Vanstone can go to Nyganda for a year. It's what he needs. Do him good to get away from London and a big teaching hospital and find out how the other half lives. I sent him for three weeks earlier this summer, but it wasn't long enough. I could see that as soon as he came back. He won't like going again, but it'll do him the world of good.'

'I can't quite see him in Nyganda, I must say,' Colegate remarked. 'Altogether too smooth for that sort of life, if you get me. Now Bill Barham – he seems cut out for it –

yet they all say his period there has been a failure.'

'Rubbish – of course, he blotted his copybook over the nurses' selection, poor fellow. Matron's furious.' He smiled reminiscently. 'Nurses' selection's a minor matter, though,' he said comfortably. Miss Glossop would have heard him with renewed fury. 'These doctors,' as she was always saying. 'Barham's done wonders in Nyganda during this year. Stirred them all up. Innovations. He has immense energy, you know, and he's tremendously capable – and a better physician than Vanstone, though both of them would be surprised to hear it. I'll tell you another thing. Taussig's going to be at least as good as Vanstone in a year or two. Hope I'll be here to see it, but I'm afraid I may not last that long.'

Colegate exclaimed.

'No good shutting your eyes to facts,' Ramsay said inexorably. 'I've had one coronary. When I have another I'll be done for. More whisky?' He poured generous glasses, as usual. 'I tell myself it keeps me arteries flexible,' he remarked ironically. 'At least it keeps me placid, and that's something. No, my days are numbered, no good blinking it. Keep an eye on Taussig for me,

243

after I've gone. He's his own worst enemy, and people don't care for him, y'know. They should see him in the wards, though. He's a different man. Humane, imaginative, understanding. He has great compassion. His patients trust him. What's more, they'll sometimes get well for him, for no apparent reason, and when they almost certainly wouldn't for anyone else. That's a great gift, and very few people have it, but when you meet it, it's unmistakable. He's good with the dying, too. He eases them out of life gently. No clever stuff. He'll see to my passing, I've laid that on. There's no one I'd sooner trust. While there's hope he'll make the most of any chances I may have, and when hope's gone he'll see me out painlessly. No damn scientific nonsense. You know what I mean.'

Their eyes met bleakly, without pretence, and spoke.

'Give me Barham or Taussig any day, if I was ill, even only with a touch of influenza,' Ramsay said, bringing the conversation firmly back to more mundane levels. 'But Vanstone has always been able to impress the pundits. The trouble is, lately he's been managing to impress himself too. His difficulty, it's always seemed to me, is that he's been consistently brilliant. From a boy. He hasn't had to live with his mistakes, and he has no understanding of failure. That's what's holding him back now. He's remote from his patients, he doesn't get on the same wave-length at all. He lacks humanity.'

'Part of this is what I could see, and what worried me.'

'Yes. I'm afraid it's been more noticeable lately. That's one reason why I sent him to Nyganda. I thought it might shake him.'

'And did it?'

'Not a bit of it. I wanted to see what he'd do if he was faced with a vast unmanageable problem. That'll stop you being so cocky and clever, young fellow, I thought.'

'But it didn't?'

'No. As far as I can see, he simply insulated himself and shrugged off all personal responsibility. Far from the experience affecting him, he merely selected a small and absolutely manageable portion of it, dealt with that most effectively, and came home delighted with himself. He seems psychologically untouched.'

'Looks to me, you know, as if your hopes for him may be doomed,' Colegate suggested, not without pleasure. He disliked Michael Vanstone more and more. 'It sounds to me as if he's one of these bright chaps who are clever sixth-formers, clever students, bright young hopefuls all along the line, with everyone thoroughly used to saying they've a brilliant future ahead. Then one day you wake up and realise they should have achieved something by now. There they are, in middle age, immature as the day they qualified. They've a mediocre future behind them, and that's their lot.'

'Michael has it in him to do better than that. If he could only let life live him, instead of dealing himself out carefully assessed doses at carefully regulated intervals, it might be the making of him. A year in Nyganda might do it. If not, then you're right, and it's too late. But he's a good lad, and I'd like to help him.'

'Even if you have to push him kicking and screaming into the future?'

'Won't be the first time I've taken my young men by the scruff of the neck and booted them out of the Central and the safe life they think they're doing so well in.' He sighed. 'Vanstone has one disappointment in store for him, which he won't like. I'm rather afraid he's counting on it. He thinks he's going to get the Chair when I retire, and he's not.'

Colegate whistled. 'That's a turn-up for the books. I've gathered that the betting's fairly high that he will.'

'Well, he won't. Not if I have anything to do with it.'

'Don't give me that. Everyone knows that you have a hell of a lot to do with it.'

'They haven't started ignoring me yet,' Ramsay admitted, in a grumbling tone. 'Though I daresay they soon will. But at the moment I think I may be said to have some small influence...'

'Don't be affected, Alec,' Murray said rudely.

Ramsay snorted. 'I was, wasn't I? I'm often pompous these days, I catch myself at it now and again. But it goes down well, you know. When there's no one like you around. And usually there isn't. Occupational disease.'

'I daresay. What about the Chair? Who *are* you backing, if it isn't Vanstone?'

'I'd like Barham to get it, myself. Afraid I may not pull it off, though.'

'They've all been saying he's out of the running.'

'Simply because of the nurses' selection mix-up? Rubbish. That happened because he was trying to do too much, and not

247

supervising the clerical staff. He knows better now. He won't make that mistake again. Personally I find that entire episode completely understandable. He does tend to take on too much, of course. He has too much heart, and he's an enthusiast.'

'But the Department of Medicine at the Central – can you trust that to an enthusiast with too much heart?'

'Ah, there you have it. That's what they'll all say. For myself, I don't think it matters. Damn it, we've got enough of the scientific approach – there are all the other Chairs – pathology, bacteriology, immunology, organic chemistry... I could go on as long as you let me. We want the art of medicine taught as well as the science, you know. That's a very old-fashioned approach these days, of course. I'd never get the Chair myself now – Vanstone'd get it away from me, eh? But I want Barham to have it, and I shall try to bring them round to my way of thinking. He cares about Nyganda. Vanstone doesn't – even you've seen that. That's what finally decided me against him. In my opinion, Barham could do something for the Central.'

'Most of them seem to think Vanstone could.'

'Oh, he could. He could. I don't deny it.

He'd keep the academic standard high – might raise it, even. But that's not of the first importance.'

'Heresy,' Murray said. 'Unsound unsound.'

Ramsay chuckled. 'There you have it,' he said. 'I'm like Barham myself. I know where we are needed. Part of our future – the future of the Central – lies out in Nyganda. That seems to me the biggest thing we've started, post-war. That's building for the future. Ikerobe is not the only new teaching hospital in Africa, by any means. But it's the one we started, and I want a good job made of it. Barham cares. What if he is an enthusiast, a bit of an opportunist, even? They are the people who start things, who sometimes make history. Not the quiet, correct, weigh it all up and shall we have a committee and a plan a small trial lot. We don't need brilliance. All we want is a perfectly ordinary chap who can get things done, and who can imbue the Nygandans with a sense of personal responsibility and devotion to an ideal.'

'And that's how you see Barham?'

'Roughly, yes. After all, I'm very ordinary myself, and I haven't done too badly. Academic brilliance is very far from being enough. Vanstone can take his clever academic mind to Nyganda, and we'll see what comes back, eh? And that'll give our two young women a breathing space, if nothing else. No doubt they'll make up their own minds about him in whatever damn fool way they choose – as they're bound to do anyway, of course. Blast it, the young devil must have something, if both Jenny and your Anne have gone overboard for him?'

'Women,' Colegate muttered disparagingly, as an answer.

'Anyway, we can give them a bit of time, and do Vanstone a bit of good as well – however much against his will. I'll send him off to Nyganda.'

Murray Colegate laughed, a low, amused sound. 'You know,' he remarked, 'it never struck me before. We are the old men now, arranging things, and lives. Behind the scenes.'

Chapter 9

On Monday morning Michael Vanstone found himself having an extremely unpleasant interview with Ramsay. He had never lied to him, and it did not occur to him to do so now. He agreed that he had been taking Jennifer out, though he asserted, with some self-satisfaction (which infuriated Ramsay) that he had ceased to do so. He had decided, he said, that the situation was not fair to her. He admitted that he had also been taking Anne Heseltine out, and that he was in fact in love with her.

Ramsay didn't like it at all.

'Why did you ever let this affair with Jenny arise, if you were already involved with Anne? There must have been something between you and Jenny – you can't break off with anyone unless there's something there to break. Damn it, you aren't an inexperienced boy. I always thought I could rely on you to look after Jenny. After all, you've known her since she was seven or eight.' The old man sighed heavily, and stared broodingly out of the window. Michael had abused his trust. He tried to be scrupulously fair to him, but he found it difficult. He reminded himself that in all probability Jennifer herself had made the running, but, as he reiterated, he had relied on Michael to handle anything like this. 'You could always have mentioned it to me, if you couldn't manage her,' he pointed out. 'I think I may say I would have understood.'

Michael knew this to be true. He was not able, however, to explain to Ramsay the full extent of Jennifer's pursuit. He was afraid to divulge the exact nature of his own affair with her. He could not bear to impart knowledge that would hurt the old man so much, he told himself. But there was more to it than this. Somehow it didn't sound too good, put baldly. 'Yes, I seduced your daughter, and I have been doing so regularly this summer. Such a sweet girl. No, I don't want to marry her. I want to marry Anne Heseltine.'

No, none of this could be said. He was ashamed that he could not tell Ramsay the truth, but resentful, too, that he should be expected to carry the entire responsibility. Blast it, Jennifer was not a complete child, as her father seemed to imagine. She had played her part. Why this out-of-date attitude that she should be looked after, protected from life? About time she grew up.

He came away from the difficult interview with a chip on his shoulder, and painfully disillusioned. He had never thought, in all the years he had known Ramsay, that he would have had it in him to be so vindictive.

For Ramsay had decided that while they were having this uncomfortable but straight talk, it was only fair to be honest about the Chair of Medicine. He would make it clear that Michael had not his backing as a candidate. Unless he told him this now, he thought, Michael might later assume that Ramsay had dropped him after their disagreement over Jennifer. He hoped that he would never be guilty of this sort of vicious revenge. In any case, it was only right to let the boy know where he stood. He might otherwise be counting on his support.

Ramsay had let his opinion emerge, unmistakably. As far as he was concerned, his candidate for the Chair was Barham.

Michael had been more shocked than he cared to show. It had never occurred to him in the past that he lacked Ramsay's support, and it did not occur to him now. Ramsay was switching to another candidate to punish him. He was not only miserably disappointed – and amazed – to see the Chair of Medicine visibly remove itself from his horizon and transfer itself to Barham's, he was also horrified to learn that Ramsay, of all people, could be so malicious. Ramsay had also mentioned his plan for Michael to go to Nyganda for a year, and he knew that this, too, was a punishment.

Hard enough to take his medicine, to face the shattered remnants of his career – transformed in half an hour. More bitter still to see Ramsay, his former chief, of whom he had been so fond, whom he had thought of as a friend, in a new and ugly light.

He sat in his consulting-room, frowning at his desk. Should he refuse to go to Nyganda? If his prospects of the Chair were ended, why fit in with Ramsay's plans? After all, no one could force him to go to the wretched country and stay there for a year. Though he refused to admit it to himself, the prospect of a long period in that primitive place frightened him. He loathed life on safari. He hated makeshifts. He knew he would feel inadequate medically and temperamentally. It was not at all his *milieu*. He knew, too, that he would be uncomfortable throughout his stay. He particularly disliked discomfort.

He broke off his unpleasant reverie to walk across to the Central for a ward round. He strode along from Wimpole Street ignoring passers-by, grim-faced, remote. He was thinking of all that had changed since he last visited the wards, of all that he had given up. A faint feeling of nobility began to grow, as he rounded Cavendish Square. It increased as he walked along Margaret Street and cut through Soho to reach Bedford Square. All this was for Anne Heseltine. He was paying a far higher price for her love than he had imagined would be demanded of him, but at least he was capable of this. Here he had risen to the need. He would see the Chair go to Barham, he was prepared to leave his satisfying, rewarding London life and struggle in Nyganda, that undeveloped backwater. There had been no hesitation in his mind, he had never attempted to compromise. All this for Anne Heseltine.

The shock he received when he joined his registrar was as agonising and unexpected as that he had received from Ramsay earlier in the morning.

'Have you heard,' Wooldridge asked, 'the news about Dr Barham?' He had been rehearsing this opening sentence to himself, and it came out self-consciously. The hospital was, as usual, seething with gossip. Wooldridge did not like to think of Vanstone finding himself, at morning coffee, in the midst of conversation about Bill and Anne's marriage, with no previous warning, and a dozen pairs of keen eyes watching to see how he took the news.

For a moment Michael thought Ramsay's blow about the Chair must already be out and round the hospital. Surely it couldn't be? But Wooldridge was continuing on different lines.

'He's marrying again, at last,' Derek said, and paused for strength to utter the final words. He thought now they could not be unexpected to Vanstone. He looked dreadful. White and aloof. Almost certainly in pain. Derek decided he must already know the truth, and be taking it far harder than they had any of them imagined he would. What about Jennifer, in that case? Did this mean that Vanstone had, after all, been serious about Anne?

'Marrying Anne Heseltine,' he now brought out, and began in his confusion to gabble. 'Quite soon, I believe – before Colegate leaves for Australia, they say – and then apparently they've having a honeymoon on the Adriatic – or so I understand.'

Michael cut him short.

'Perhaps you could defer your speculation as to their exact destination until we have seen our patients, Wooldridge,' he enunciated cuttingly. 'I am afraid the details are rather less fascinating to me than they appear to be to you. Once we have attended to the small matter of those requiring our care, you will be entirely free to devote your attention to the prospect of where Barham will spend his honeymoon and in what hotel. You may, if you so desire, consult the rail and air time-tables and work out a suitable itinerary for them. In the meantime, if you don't mind...'

He then conducted a ward round which was as terrifying an hour as any of them – not only Wooldridge, but the house physician, the students, sister, the nurses, and indeed, the patients – had known.

'The examiners for the membership will be nothing to me now,' Wooldridge said afterwards. 'No examiner will ever succeed in terrorising me again. I survived this morning with Vanstone. I'll never be able to make a bigger fool of myself, nor ever be shown up more icily.'

'You weren't alone, I gather,' his friend, Marlow's registrar, pointed out, by way of comfort.

'No, indeed, we all got it in the neck, including sister. Who would have thought the poor old devil would mind so much? If I didn't feel sure he'd only bite my head off again, I'd go and try and do a bit of mopping up. But I don't think he wants to see me much – I don't think I bring relief, somehow.' He had smiled ruefully. 'I think instead I'd better go and mop up the patients. He was quite brutal with poor old Benson, the muscular dystrophy in the end bed.'

Michael would have liked to be brutal with everyone. A fine fool he had made of himself. Anne, too. No doubt she had been laughing at him throughout the summer, playing with him. And he had given up everything for her. If only he had known, before he had seen Ramsay this morning, about Anne and Bill. Then he need have told Ramsay nothing. He could have said he was unable to understand what he was talking about, that of course... Sickened with himself, he had turned away from this line of thought. He would not have lied like this, for the Chair of Medicine, surely?

No. But he could have played his cards differently, have been more cautious. He need not have blurted out the facts. Quite unnecessary, that. He need not have exposed himself in so unflattering a light. He had felt he owed Ramsay the truth. But here he had been naïve. He had dealt with Ramsay with integrity, but what an exhibition he had made of himself, and what a price he had paid. He had lost the Chair, he had already lost Anne – and presumably Jennifer, too. They were all gloating over his discomfiture. Even Wooldridge, whom he had always imagined to be loyal to him, had been gloating, had enjoyed telling him the news so that he could watch how he took it, and have a tale to relate in the common-room.

By day he was angry, and blamed everyone but himself. In the dead of night it was different. Then, wakeful and alone, he knew that he had lost something very precious. And this time he didn't mean the Chair of Medicine.

He had no knowledge of the scene at the Summer Ball. It did not cross his mind – and no one was ever to tell him – that Anne had discovered his affair with Jennifer. But he knew well enough that throughout the summer he had been divided in his mind. He thought now, looking back, that he might not have lost Anne if he had been wholehearted in his love for her. Alone at night, he knew that he had been weighing her in the balance against the Chair (with Jennifer more or less sitting in it, he thought bitterly, though this had not been apparent to him at the time – or had it?) But he knew, when he faced himself in these cold moments of truth, that everything had been his own doing. He had never given himself to Anne. He had played around, and had assumed that what he offered would be enough to win her.

Evidently he had over-estimated himself. While he could not quite forgive her for her inability to recognise his worth – how could any woman of perception prefer the glib Barham to himself? – he knew the chief responsibility was his own. He had believed himself to be so much more able – to put it at its lowest – than the rest of them, yet when the test came, he had been wholly unequal to it. So much for him.

To face his own disaster was a shock. He had never imagined that he could fail. Failure, he had always thought, was for others, the mediocrities, men like Barham. He had pitied them. Men of outstanding merit, and this was how he had always seen himself, did not meet with real defeat. They might be worsted now and again, though not often, in what might be termed minor skirmishes. However, no one could reasonably suggest his present defeats were minor. He had lost Anne, and he had lost the Chair of Medicine. Both were vitally important to him. He might even have faced the necessity to forgo one in order to attain the other. But to lose both? This was self-evident failure, irretrievable and final. He had bungled his own life, that was what it came to. He had only himself to thank.

This, of course, was the opinion at the Central, too. The hospital was delighted with the engagement between Bill and Anne. They made a fine couple. They were all highly amused at Vanstone's discomfiture. They thought – like Michael himself – that Anne Heseltine had pulled a fast one on him, and that it served him right. He had been far too self-confident.

They were pleased, in addition, to hear that he was to go to Nyganda. They knew he would hate it, and, with Ramsay, they considered it would do him the world of good.

Ramsay, as it happened, was wondering if he had been too hard on Michael Vanstone. They had had their talk on the Monday morning. Early the same afternoon Colegate had telephoned to tell him about Anne's engagement to Bill Barham, and to recommend a policy of masterly inactivity regarding Michael and Jennifer.

'Too late. I've already had it out with him.'

'Aow. I should never have got so steamed up about him and Anne – must have been on the wrong lines (who'd be a father, eh, Alec?) I'm afraid I misled you. May have been very unfair to Vanstone, poor beggar.'

Ramsay did not tell him that he had not misled him, that Michael had admitted to loving Anne, to wishing to marry her. He thought this news would help no one, least of all Vanstone, it appeared. Poor chap. He would keep his secret for him.

He congratulated Colegate on having Anne settled to his satisfaction ('you're one father who should be fairly easy in his mind, at any rate'), and he and Isobel invited the Colegates and the engaged couple to dinner – one of many similar celebrations.

Ramsay had the greatest difficulty in preventing his wife from inviting Michael to his dinner to partner Jennifer. He did not think it desirable to pass on to Isobel his discoveries about Michael, as he could not rely on her discretion. He had never been able to do so. It was not that Isobel was in any way malicious, or even an inveterate gossip. But she inevitably blurted out, in the most unsuitable company, highly embarrassing comments on people or events. Comments that should never have been made, and could only have been made if she had access to confidential disclosures. As a young man, Ramsay had been unable to prevent himself from telling her his inner thoughts, his worries and his plans. But a few of her *gaffes* had cured him of this habit. As a result he had no one at home with whom to share his anxieties and his triumphs, but he had grown accustomed to this. Accustomed, too, to laying down the law in his family circle, and being obeyed without question. As he was obeyed now.

'I don't want Michael or Jennifer at this dinner,' he said briefly.

'But Alec–'

'I don't want them, Isobel. Don't invite them.'

'I don't see why–'

'I won't have either of them.'

'No, dear. Now, who shall we have?'

'I leave it to you,' he replied unfairly.

The dinner, as it turned out, was a success. Ramsay ordered champagne, so Isobel cancelled the Spanish burgundy, and even substituted – extravagantly, she felt – turkey for the saddle of mutton she had planned. Since in Isobel's system of catering, mutton was eaten with boiled potatoes, cabbage and mint sauce, while turkey involved roast potatoes, Brussels sprouts, crisp rolls of bacon, sausages, two sorts of stuffing, bread sauce – in fact, all the trimmings, as though it had been Christmas – the improvement was considerable. The next course remained baked apples – Isobel had brought a hamper of windfalls up from Haslemere – but even these were accompanied by cream instead of the usual custard. 'It'll mean a big increase in the milk bill,' she grumbled to her husband, 'but after all, it *is* a celebration.'

Everyone was celebrating except Michael Vanstone, it seemed. Ramsay was sorry for him, but there was nothing he could do to alter the facts. Nothing could be undone. Vanstone could not be offered the Chair of Medicine as a consolation prize, nor should he be encouraged to remain in London instead of going to Nyganda. The old man wished he had not spoken to him so harshly, when he had this heavy blow awaiting him. He considered, though, that the whole unhappy affair might be the making of him. He knew that at present Michael was taking his loss badly, but he would work through this initial reaction, and then, as he said to Colegate, 'we shall see what stuff he's made of.'

This was what they all thought at the Central. This was how the gossip ran – in the residents' common-room, in the nurses' home, and over the dinner tables. 'Now we'll see what he's made of,' they told each other.

Just as they had become accustomed to this idea, the picture changed.

One afternoon, Ramsay had his second heart attack, on the stairs between Jenner and the X-ray department. This time he did not survive. Within a couple of hours the news was all over the hospital. Uncle Alex was dead. His friendly presence, wreathed in smoke from his inevitable pipe, had gone from them. Nearly everyone felt a sense of personal loss. Alec Ramsay had been loved at the Central.

It fell to Michael to break the news, first to Isobel Ramsay, and then, at her request, to Jennifer. She was broken-hearted. She had adored her father, and was totally demoralised by his sudden departure from her life. She turned without hesitation to Michael for comfort, and he could not bear to fail her.

Isobel Ramsay, too, found his assistance invaluable, and had no reason to doubt his willingness to give it. He was a great support to them both in the days that followed, and became like a son of the house.

What else could he do? He knew inescapably that this time he would not get away. It hardly seemed to matter very much any longer. He experienced a faint intermittent hope, of which he was ashamed, that at least he might after all get the Chair.

Isobel Ramsay left him to make all the arrangements for her – the funeral, the memorial service, the dealings with the solicitors and the bank. She decided, after a great deal of talk, to sell Densworth, and asked Michael to find agents and arrange for the sale or both house and furniture. He would not mind seeing to everything, would he? As far as she was concerned, the place was to be disposed of. The rest she left to him. The house would be much too large for her alone – and Jennifer, she added archly, 'will soon be making other plans.' She looked meaningly at him, and he evaded her glance. More was to follow. '*She* won't be living at home much longer.'

Isobel referred to her expectations more than once. 'It's the greatest comfort to me,

Michael, that you are here to look after Jennifer. Otherwise I should be *most* worried about her. Because as you know, she did adore Alec. Now, however...' Another meaning look.

Remarks of this sort were made several times daily. She also began offering him furniture. 'If there's anything you think you might need, Michael, you must take it, of course.' She made him go round the house with Jennifer and herself before the inventory was taken. He found it a depressing pilgrimage. When they reached Ramsay's study it became unbearable. But here Jennifer banged the door shut. 'Not now,' she said. 'Some other time.' Her voice was thick with tears. Even Isobel respected her misery, and led the way briskly to the kitchen, saying it was time for a cup of tea, they were all exhausted.

Arrived in the kitchen, she had what struck her at once as a brilliant idea.

'I know,' she said. 'I know who will want to buy the house. Dr Barham.' She paused for approbation, which she failed to obtain. Jennifer paid no attention, merely answering, 'Oh, um, d'you think so?' while turning the taps on and off over the sink, where she was crying quietly, her back to the two of them.

'But of course,' Isobel cried. 'It's an inspiration. Isn't it, Michael?'

He muttered furiously.

'What? What? I can't hear what you say – Jennifer, do for heaven's sake stop playing about with the taps like that, I can't hear myself think, and I can't hear a word Michael says.'

'Just as well,' Michael murmured to himself. He would have liked to beat her over the head with the nearest saucepan. At this moment Jennifer turned off the water, and Isobel heard him.

She interpreted his remark to her own satisfaction. 'Michael agreed with me,' she announced triumphantly. 'Well, will you talk to him?' she demanded.

Michael hedged. 'I don't know,' he said feebly, 'if–'

'Of course he'll be delighted,' Isobel stated confidently. 'I know they're looking for a house.'

This news gave Michael no pleasure.

'You go and see him, and tell him he can have this. Bring him down to see it,' she continued indefatigably. 'Bring them both down. Anne will want to have a good look round. You and Jenny can show them everything.' She beamed delightedly. 'I'll stay in

London, they won't want me as well. I'll have a little rest. You and Jenny bring them down, and you can all have a meal here together. Cold ham,' she suggested encouragingly, and walked over to her store cupboard. 'Or there are some tins of corned beef that want using up.'

'I'm afraid I couldn't possibly take another day off,' Michael said irritably, and with desperation. But it was true. He had taken over Ramsay's private practice, in addition to his own, and his days were full. In any case, they were short-staffed at the Central without Ramsay, short of senior men. This had justified one of his first decisions, soon taken. He would not go to Nyganda. To remain in London was only reasonable. For one thing, what hope would he have of the Chair, stuck out in Ikerobe, away from the lobbying and manoeuvring? It would be difficult to spare a consultant for a year in Nyganda now, and Michael used his influence to prove it unnecessary. One of the registrars could go.

Andy Taussig went. Just as well, they all said. After all, he had made the Central too hot to hold him at last. For it had been Andy who had found Ramsay after his heart attack. The gossip that if he had been quicker, had summoned the cardiac resuscitation team immediately, the old man's life might have been saved. Of course, it might not have been for long, his heart had been in a bad state. They agreed that he had only a short span of days ahead of him. To live on as an invalid...?

'Taussig should have jumped to it.'

'After all, every second counts, in a case like that. Four minutes is the longest you've got, and...'

'But he says Ramsay was already dead when he found him.'

'Open heart massage, within four minutes.'

'Come to that, even external massage...'

'Did he do *anything?*'

'After all, this is a teaching hospital, surely we can lay on cardiac resuscitation as quickly as anyone?'

'But if he was dead when Taussig found him...'

'Yes, indeed, worse than useless to have worked on him then.'

'He wouldn't have wanted that – we all know what he said about that.'

'And after all, the survival rate, after a second coronary...'

'How many ever leave the ward, even if

you do get them round?'

'Surely Taussig should have tried, though? After all, this is a teaching hospital.'

So the gossip went, round in circles, back to the same point. Andy made no attempt to defend himself. When they asked, 'Are you *sure* it was too late?' he answered only, 'Any time would be too late. That's what he said himself.' For Andy had kept faith with Ramsay, as the old man had known he would, whatever the cost. 'When my time comes, see that they let me go in peace,' he had told his registrar. 'I don't want to lie in the wards, an inanimate hulk strung up to a lot of damned tubes, while they try to keep my circulation going, and hope that if they can it'll be in time for it to be worth while. I don't want to live on as a vegetable.' This had been his great fear, and Andy had respected it. Ramsay could have found no one better. For Andy knew at first hand that a man might find life not worth the living, he understood the wish to depart in peace at the appointed time. And he had the strength to maintain his conviction, not only in the face of criticism, unpopularity, pressure, but in the face of death itself.

But Andy was desolate, though they none of them suspected it. He had determined years ago to care nothing for anyone, but now he found he had loved his chief, that kindly, compassionate old man. Uncle Alec, as they had all affectionately called him. Andy, though he had lost his own family twenty years earlier, found that he still had close ties, whose breaking cut as deeply as ever. In his loneliness he turned instinctively to Meg. He telephoned to her in Ikerobe.

She took the next plane back to him. To her he poured it all out, his loneliness, his sadness, and at last his need for her. He had never admitted it before, either to himself or to her. He shook with inexplicable terror as he told her the truth, and clung to her desperately. Meg cradled him in her arms and loved him. They were closer than ever. The past ten years, as it turned out, had been merely a prelude. Their real life together was beginning now.

'Andy and I are more in love than ever,' Meg told Anne, sitting down on her bed, and kicking off her shoes. They had both been shopping for clothes for Anne's wedding, and had returned to the Hampstead house for dinner, where they were to be joined by Andy and Bill, who were coming from the Central together. 'It was worth all the agony, and all the loneliness in Ikerobe, to get where we have somehow – Lord knows how – arrived at last. I can't think how we ever imagined we could separate,' she added. 'I must have been mad. But it all seemed to have gone so wrong, and I hadn't the energy any more to cope with him.'

Anne swivelled round from the dressing-table, where she had been about to try on once again the enormous hat in which, they had hilariously decided, it would be sensational for Anne to be married. 'You were worn out,' she said. 'And no wonder.'

'But I *wasn't* worn out,' Meg retorted. 'That was what was so odd. For the first time in years I wasn't overworked and short of sleep, and that's when it all began to go wrong. Nothing seemed worthwhile, Andy least of all. I think this house had something to do with it. I hate it. We ought to sell it, only it's an additional complication. Anyway, Andy likes it. And he's got enough to think about at the moment, what with having been Uncle Alec's registrar and having to hand everything over to Michael, as well as getting ready for Nyganda. Michael seems to have fallen on his feet, doesn't he? Trust him. He's not only inherited Uncle Alec's private practice – well worth having, that, all sorts of *top people–*' she giggled. 'Michael'll love that.

He's also got Uncle Alec's beds at the Central, and I expect the Chair of Medicine, too. And no doubt Jennifer into the bargain, though she's hardly an acquisition.'

'We oughtn't to be too hard on her – she's only young and silly.'

'Hard as nails. I wish Michael joy of her. I only hope he's pleased with himself, that's all. But he would never have done for you – you do realise that, don't you? I mean, you wouldn't be so dotty as to go and marry Bill if you were still hankering after Michael, would you?' She gave Anne a penetrating glare.

Anne laughed, easily, with genuine amusement. 'There's no need to look so ferocious,' she said. 'You look prepared to cancel everything at the point of a gun, if necessary. It's all right. I'm not marrying Bill on the rebound.'

'As long as you're sure.'

'I'm more sure about Bill than I've been about anything in my whole life. Bill suits me, you know. We're so comfortable together. I can't believe we're getting married next week – I feel as if we've been married for years. It seems impossible that next week there's going to be a big pompous wedding – it's so inappropriate, somehow. That's why

I'm not excited at all.'

'No, I noticed you weren't. I was hoping it didn't mean you were depressed. Except that I could see you were far from miserable. More smug.'

'Yes, that's how I feel. Smug and tranquil. Easy in my mind – I don't think I've ever been that before.'

'That *is* what matters. I daresay you won't believe me – I'm sure no one at the Central would – but all the time I've been married to Andy, except when we were actually in the middle of one of our rows, I've been easy in my mind. It was only when we separated that I felt peculiar. Lost. As if something awful was going to happen to me at any moment.'

'That's rather how I felt with Michael. Only I didn't understand what it was at the time. I was edgy and didn't know why. I still don't know exactly why. But I think it must have been what you said, earlier, was true. We were wrong for each other. If I'd married him – not that I think there was much chance of that, I agree with you, he isn't the sort of man to contemplate marriage except for what you might call excellent administrative reasons. Never for love. But if I *had* married him, I expect I should have gone on feeling like that all the time. Because I should never have known where I was with him. Never have been sure of him. (How right I would have been.) Never have known what he was up to, what he wanted, what he was feeling, fundamentally, deep down. And either I should have gone on worrying and trying to make contact and keep it – only I'm not very good at that sort of thing. I'm too *like* Michael for that, I need someone like Bill to do it to *me* – or I should have given up the struggle, and we would simply have co-existed politely – very politely, I'm sure, knowing Michael – on parallel lines that could never meet.'

'It's odd about Michael – there he is, handsome, brilliantly clever (let's face it, every young girl's dream) with all life's material rewards being handed to him on a plate. Yet you and I have to go and pick a couple of twirps who are apparently going to spend their lives in the jungle, rather than the brilliant future Professor, and what's more we know why and we know we're dead right. Michael's missed out somewhere along the line on the one thing that really matters.'

'He's not an utter phoney,' Anne protested. 'He'll find someone, eventually, who'll be able to do something for him, who will really matter to him.'

'No, he won't,' Meg said flatly. 'He'll marry Jennifer, and they'll have a highly polished successful life together. But both of them will be untouched by anything approaching reality.'

Anne had wandered over to the window, and stood looking down, playing with the blind cord. She chuckled. 'Our realities are approaching now,' she announced. There was the sound of car doors slamming, and Andy and Bill, engaged, as was clearly apparent, in some furious argument, opened the tall gate and came across the patio.

Meg had joined Anne and watched them both.

'Never a dull moment,' she murmured, her lips curving with affection. 'They're having a row. We'd better go down and referee.'

The row was, it seemed, about the correct treatment for an old lady recently admitted with cor pulmonale, with fascinating complications. She had been Ramsay's case, and so under Andy's care, and they had treated her conservatively, in view of her frailty and advanced age. Now she had come under Vanstone, who wanted to put her into one of his trials of a new drug. Andy was against this – and so, it turned out, was Bill. But they kept advancing arguments on Michael's behalf, and becoming heated as they took it in turns to demolish them. The discussion had soon left the old lady, and had become theoretic and philosophical. But it was not handled philosophically by either Andy or Bill, but rather with passion and fury.

Meg and Anne had the greatest difficulty in detaching them from it sufficiently to manoeuvre them into seats at the teak table for dinner. Anne had opened the wine, after Meg had three times placed the corkscrew in Andy's hand and the bottle at his elbow. On the first occasion he had said, 'Oh, all right, yes, of course I will. But the point is, Bill, that Vanstone thinks that in the long run–'

'Yes, but the danger is that if one begins not to see the patient as an individual, but instead as part of a system of research–'

'Be fair,' Andy interjected. 'No one suggests that Vanstone ever allows himself to lose sight of–'

'No, no, but don't you see–'

Meg again proffered the corkscrew and the bottle, which by this time Andy had absent-mindedly pushed aside.

'Just a minute, Meg. Now, look, what I mean is–'

'I know perfectly well what you mean,' Andy, and what I'm trying to get across to you is, it isn't what Vanstone *thinks* he's doing that is the danger, the danger is that what he wants to achieve in the way of significant results is going to undermine his sense of what's best for each individual–'

'That's what I'm talking about. Surely you can understand that? Do you seriously suggest that I can't recognise the difference between–'

'Andy, if you could for one minute recognise this bottle and the corkscrew, we could all have a drink with our meal.'

'Why on earth didn't you say so before? This should have been opened half an hour ago, at least. It hasn't had time to breathe. Women cannot understand about wine, Bill. Don't you agree? I remember, I once got a very special, extremely expensive Volnay in. It was when the Ramsays were coming to dinner – it was wasted on them, of course, dear old Uncle Alec drank about a quart of whisky before and after. Heartrending. But I wanted to do the old man proud, and–'

'You mean you wanted to do yourself proud,' Bill interrupted. 'Don't give me that bull. And that's exactly my point. Now, look at you, a Viennese, highly intelligent and fairly subtle, brought up in Freud's own home town, a physician yourself, and you haven't the faintest notion when you lead yourself straight up the garden path.'

The conversation exploded again, and Anne took away the bottle and opened it in the kitchen.

While she was doing this, Meg suddenly offered her the house.

'You might just as well live in it. It'll simply be here, doing nothing. And you always liked it, Anne.'

'I love it.'

'Well, why not live in it? We won't be here, it'll only be empty. It will save you either buying or renting somewhere, before you come out to Nyganda next year. Then we can use it for our leave, and by that time we may know what we want to do about it – sell it or not. Andy doesn't want to sell it.'

'I must say I'd like it very much,' Anne said slowly, wondering how Bill would take to the idea. 'I'm selling my flat, as you know – it belongs too much to the past.'

'Come on, then, we'll see what Bill says.' Meg stormed into the dining-room, slammed dishes down, and announced her plan amid the clatter.

'Would you like it, Anne?' Bill asked, his attention successfully caught by Meg's crashing introduction, so that he had actually broken off his argument to listen to what she had to say.

'Yes, I must say I would. I've always loved this house, whatever Meg may say about it. I could put Mother's furniture into store, and we could look after all this for Meg and Andy.' She made a sweeping gesture with her hand, to include, apparently, the architecture, the teak, the Arne Jacobsen chairs, and the indoor plants.

'Do have it,' Meg urged them. 'Someone might as well get some pleasure out of it.'

'Yes, certainly,' Andy agreed. 'And it will remain our capital investment,' he savoured the words. 'It will increase in value while we are in Nyganda. Nothing like property for that.'

'And we'd pay you rent,' Bill pointed out. 'We'd have to work something out. I must say, this is a great deal better than Densworth.'

'Densworth?' Anne screeched. 'Who said anything about Densworth?'

'Vanstone did,' Bill said, grinning. 'It appears Isobel Ramsay thought Densworth would do nicely for you and me, and she dispatched Vanstone to make the offer. I didn't bother to tell you before, because I was so certain you wouldn't want to live there. But I had the devil's own job choking Isobel off.'

'What an absolutely hellish idea,' Anne said with feeling.

Meg began to laugh helplessly. 'I can just see you there–' she began, when the telephone rang. Andy went to answer it. 'Oh, Anne,' Meg went on, her eyes alight with amusement, 'just think of you turning into another Lady Ramsay. Think of the awful dinners you'd have to give, and that terrible drawing-room with the ghastly fireplace, and those mullioned windows factory made by Messrs Crittall–'

Andy came back. 'For you,' he said to Bill. 'It's Marlow. He wants you for a consultation, immediately if not sooner.'

'No need to look so delighted,' Bill said. 'I've never known a chap like you for thriving on the discomfort of others. You might at least try to hide it.'

Andy grinned. 'No one has ever suggested I am lacking in honesty,' he said. 'Unpopular I may be, yes.'

'I'll say. Unpopular with me right now – nearly as unpopular, but not quite, as Mar-

282

low. But you wait, I'll pay you back. Wait until we're both in Nyganda, and you're sitting comfortably with Meg, having your dinner and exchanging all the terrible local gossip there'll undoubtedly be. And a messenger will appear from me, saying come at once, and bring vast quantities of apparatus and drugs and vaccines – everything I can think of, oxygen cylinders, the lot. You'll set off, cursing and hungry, by canoe and jungle path, sweating it out, and camping, and pushing on, and reaching one village only to find I've left it for the next, and eventually you'll catch up with me after about six days bashing, and I'll scratch my head and say, "Ah, Andy, nice to see you, old boy, now what was it I wanted you for? Blessed if I can remember. Better take all that paraphernalia back to Ikerobe, my dear chap, it's no good here – oh, and take my dirty laundry at the same time, will you?"' With this parting shot he went to talk to Marlow, while Andy chuckled, and Meg said to Anne, 'Schoolboys, both of them, just schoolboys.'

As it turned out, though, Bill and Anne were not to go to Nyganda, other than for brief tours. For all Michael Vanstone's precautions, Bill was to become Professor of

Medicine – to everyone's amazement, and not least his own.

Dead, Ramsay did more for his candidate then he could have achieved in life.

A surprising number of people had been very fond of Alec Ramsay, and found themselves strangely bereft by his death. They all knew whom he wanted for the Chair. They knew, too, what Ramsay had wanted for Nyganda, and they could see that Bill wanted it too. No more fitting tribute could be paid to Ramsay than to put Bill Barham in his place, to carry on his work with the same spirit and the same values. Because they were somewhat ashamed of these deep feelings, they kept them quiet. Secretly, each of them thought that Bill had no hope of the Chair – not sound enough, my dear chap – but out of loyalty to Ramsay, one by one, each thinking he was the only one to be so sentimental, they used their influence on his behalf. When he got the Chair, they were amazed to find that their own feelings had been shared by the entire medical committee.

They were not to regret their decision, though certainly at first they were a trifle alarmed by the whirlwind they had called into being.

Before this, however, came Bill and Anne's wedding – attended, inevitably, by the entire hospital. Meg and Andy had put off their flight back to Ikerobe to be there, Miss Glossop attended, and as usual held a sort of subsidiary reception of her own, just inside the church porch on this occasion. Michael was there, well-groomed, smoother than ever, escorting the Ramsays. Lady Ramsay had managed to find herself another extraordinary hat. Jennifer, somewhat ostentatiously wearing black, had a new pale young beauty, her eyes limpid and brimming. She looked wan but gallant. As her father had said, she was a trier.

Michael was haunted. Haunted by all that had gone, by the past summer that had been so full of promise, by his hopes that were so plainly to remain unfulfilled. All that was before him now was a recurring round of duty. He determined that at least he would keep faith with this beautiful, trusting girl, who so firmly insisted on giving him her life. And who was he to turn it down? No one else wanted him, no one else admired him, as far as he could see. Jennifer was proud of him, and he could not fail to bask in the glow of her approval. He smiled sardonically, and caught her eye. She smiled back.

She had no idea what was amusing him, but she responded loyally to his mood. He took her arm, and they drew comfort from one another.

For once, though, no one was paying much attention to Michael Vanstone. All eyes were on the Colegates and Bill and Anne. Pamela Colegate's stunning creation was, fortunately, hidden by her vast mink. Murray was, as he complained, 'rigged out in all the gear I detest'.

Bill was exuberant, Anne quietly glowing. Wearing champagne silk and the great creamy straw hat that should have dwarfed her, but which in fact failed to quench her regained zest for life, she stood, slender and upright, between Murray Colegate and Bill, each clearly proud of her. Tim would have recognised his golden girl.